The Holiday _____ month as Gulliver's Travels brings together one more couple—hospital administrator JACK MERRITT and his earthy, exuberant driver, ANGIE PARETTI.

So if you've been enjoying the Holiday Honeymoons series all along—or even if this is your first time—you won't want to miss this exciting, suspenseful and romantic story by beloved author Merline Lovelace.

* * *

Here is what some of the best-loved authors in romance have had to say about Merline Lovelace:

"Strong and clever characters populate the Lovelace world in stories that sizzle with a passion for life and love."

—*New York Times* bestselling author
Nora Roberts

"Merline Lovelace's stories are filled with unforgettable characters, scintillating romance, and steeped with emotional depth. She's the brightest new star in the romance genre. Each new book is an adventure."

—Award-winning author
Debbie Macomber

Dear Reader,

Once again, you've come to the right place if you're looking for that seductive mix of romance and excitement that is quintessentially Intimate Moments. Start the month with *The Lady in Red*—by reader favorite Linda Turner. Your heart will be in your throat as rival homicide reporters Blake Nickels and Sabrina Jones see their relationship change from professional to personal— with a killer on their trail all the while. And don't miss the conclusion of the HOLIDAY HONEYMOONS miniseries, Merline Lovelace's *The 14th...and Forever*. You'll wish for a holiday—and a HOLIDAY HONEYMOON—every month of the year.

The rest of the month is fabulous, too, with new books from Rebecca Daniels: *Mind Over Marriage;* Marilyn Tracy: *Almost Perfect,* the launch book in her ALMOST, TEXAS miniseries; and Allie Harrison: *Crime of the Heart.* And welcome new author Charlotte Walker, as she debuts with *Yesterday's Bride.* Every one of these books is full of passion, and sometimes peril—don't miss a single one.

And be sure to come back next month, when the romance and excitement continue, right here in Silhouette Intimate Moments.

Enjoy!

Leslie J. Wainger
Senior Editor and Editorial Coordinator

Please address questions and book requests to:
Silhouette Reader Service
U.S.: 3010 Walden Ave., P.O. Box 1325, Buffalo, NY 14269
Canadian: P.O. Box 609, Fort Erie, Ont. L2A 5X3

# THE 14TH...
# AND
# FOREVER

## MERLINE
## LOVELACE

*Silhouette*

**INTIMATE** MOMENTS®

Published by Silhouette Books

**America's Publisher of Contemporary Romance**

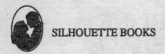 SILHOUETTE BOOKS

ISBN 0-373-07764-5

THE 14TH...AND FOREVER

Copyright © 1997 by Merline Lovelace

**Books by Merline Lovelace**

Silhouette Intimate Moments

*Somewhere in Time* #593
\*Night of the Jaguar* #637
\*The Cowboy and
  the Cossack* #657
\*Undercover Man* #669
\*Perfect Double* #692
†*The 14th...and Forever* #764

Silhouette Desire

*Dreams and Schemes* #872
†*Halloween Honeymoon* #1030
†*Wrong Bride, Right Groom* #1037

Silhouette Books

Fortune's Children
*Beauty and the Bodyguard*

\*Code Name: Danger
†Holiday Honeymoons

---

## *MERLINE LOVELACE*

As a career air force officer, Merline Lovelace served tours of duty in Vietnam, at the Pentagon and at bases all over the world. During her years in uniform she met and married her own handsome hero and stored up enough adventures to keep her fingers flying over the keyboard for years to come. When not glued to the word processor, Merline goes antiquing with her husband, Al, or chases little white balls around the golf courses of Oklahoma.

Merline loves to read and write sizzling contemporaries and sweeping historical sagas. Look for her next book, *Countess in Buckskin,* coming soon from Harlequin Historicals. She enjoys hearing from readers and can be reached via e-mail at lovelace@iamerica.net or at P.O. Box 892717, Oklahoma City, OK, 73189.

To Caren and Mike Fichtel, two people who know what love is all about. Thanks for opening your hearts and your home to Al and me so many times over the years. And thanks, Mike, for all your great insights into the exciting, adventure-filled, exotic profession of accounting.

# *Prologue*

"Good morning, Tiff."

Tiffany Tarrington Toulouse hung up her coat and returned her office manager's warm smile. "Mornin', Lucy."

A romantic to the tips of her toes, Tiffany sighed at the happiness underscoring Lucy Falco's dark-eyed beauty. The woman positively glowed since her remarriage to her former husband, Chris, last month. That their dramatic reunion had occurred right here, at Gulliver's Travels—in the middle of a New Year's Eve break-in, no less!—only added to the romance of the occasion.

That was Tiffany's considered opinion, anyway. Lucy still grimaced every time she passed the newly repaired wall that the trio of bumbling would-be safecrackers had reduced to rubble.

"Here." Lucy offered a hand-painted china mug. "I

made some tea. You'd better have a cup to thaw you out.''

''Thanks!''

The older woman took the steaming mug gratefully. A native Atlantan, she'd shivered all the way to work in this unusually chilly February weather.

''Why are you in so early?'' Lucy asked curiously. ''I thought you said you were going to treat yourself to a Valentine's Day champagne breakfast at Antoine's.''

In a feminine gesture as ageless as time, the travel agent patted her silvery curls. ''I decided to let Humphrey treat me to a champagne dinner instead. You know, for a mere boy of fifty-one, he has definite possibilities.''

''I'm glad,'' Lucy replied, her black eyes dancing. ''Our agency seems to be specializing in holiday honeymoons lately. Maybe the next romantic trip you arrange will be yours.''

''Maybe.'' Tiffany's smug smile faded. ''In the meantime, though, I came in early to cancel the arrangements I made for Dr. Merritt.''

''Well, I tried to warn you he wouldn't want that Valentine's Day getaway package you put together for him,'' Lucy said gently. ''Penthouse suites and stretch limos aren't his style. You know how he insists on no frills when he travels on business.''

''But he never goes anywhere unless it's on business! We've been handling travel arrangements for the employees of Children's Hospital for years now, and Dr. Merritt has yet to take a vacation. Besides, I wanted to do something to show our appreciation for the way he got Jimmy's daughter into that special asthma clinic.''

''He's the chief financial officer at the hospital, Tiff, responsible for audits and fraud investigations and such.

He, of all people, can't appear to be living extravagantly or wasting the hospital's travel funds on limousines."

"I know, I know." The older woman's eyes twinkled. "But auditor or not, the man makes this slightly used heart of mine go bumpety-bump every time I deliver tickets to his office. I was hoping a silver limo, some chilled champagne and a view of Washington D.C. in lights might make him forget his facts and figures and bottom lines for a while. Who knows? He might have found someone interesting to share this Valentine's Day with, after all."

"He's going up to D.C. on business," Lucy repeated firmly. "He'll probably be in meetings the whole time he's there. You'd better follow his instructions and cancel those reservations."

"I will." Tiffany heaved a huge, melodramatic sigh. "But what a waste of the most romantic night of the year!"

# Chapter 1

Jack saw her the moment he walked out of the terminal.

She was leaning against the fender of a midnight-blue sedan parked illegally in the drop-off lane, hugging a book to her chest. With her eyes closed, her face tipped up to the thin February sunshine, and a river of glossy chestnut curls spilling down her neck, she was completely oblivious of the noisy airport bustle.

She looked, Jack decided, like a pagan goddess worshiping the first faint hint of spring.

Since he wasn't a man who usually indulged in flights of fantasy, the whimsical thought surprised him...as did the little kick of pleasure the sight of her stirred. It was an instinctive and purely masculine reaction, the uncomplicated enjoyment a healthy male takes in the sight of an intriguing female. It was also one he hadn't experienced in a long time, he realized ruefully. Too long. Not since his divorce five years ago, anyway.

He'd been working too hard, Jack decided. And worrying too much about this damned testimony.

Muscles already stiff from the bumpy flight from Atlanta twisted into even tighter knots at the thought of the Senate subcommittee he'd face the day after tomorrow. He was scheduled to meet with the powerful chairman of the subcommittee in less than an hour to go over the thrust of his testimony. Which meant Jack had less than an hour to decide just what the hell he was going to say.

He shifted his briefcase to his left hand, already burdened with his carryon and trench coat, and rubbed the back of his neck. In a deliberate effort to ease his tightly coiled tension, he allowed his gaze to drift back to the sun worshiper.

Her thick, curling mane would have snared any man's attention, tumbling as it did over the shoulders of a smartly tailored black tunic trimmed with a double row of gold buttons. The tunic was paired with a slim skirt slit on one side to reveal a discreet and thoroughly tantalizing stretch of curving, black-stockinged calf. Her high-topped sneakers decorated with glittery red hearts should have looked incongruous with the rest of her elegant attire. Instead, they added a touch that made more than one observer smile, Jack included.

At that moment, a capricious gust of wind whooshed along the terminal walkway and jerked her from her enjoyment of the sun. It also, Jack couldn't help noticing, lifted the flap of her skirt.

Nice.

Very nice.

He was contemplating how quickly simple masculine enjoyment could flare into something a whole lot more complex when she shivered and caught his gaze. Her sable brows lifted in feminine amusement.

He deserved that, Jack admitted. He'd been staring at her like a gawky teen. His only defense was that the woman was eminently starable. Giving her a grin that tried for apologetic but probably fell short by a few degrees, he turned away.

"Dr. Merritt?"

His grin slipped, then froze in place. The tension that traveled with him like a second shadow these days snapped back into place. Instantly and immediately wary, he turned to face her.

She pushed away from the fender. The amusement was gone. In its place was a look of polite inquiry.

"Dr. Jack Merritt?"

As vice president and chief financial officer of the nonprofit Children's Hospital, Jack worked daily with a host of consulting physicians and an ever-increasing patient population. To avoid confusion, he never used the titles he'd earned along with his string of business degrees. Titles didn't interest him, in any case.

What did interest him was what this woman wanted with him.

"I'm Jack Merritt," he confirmed slowly.

She tossed the book she'd been holding through the open passenger window and strolled toward him with an easy, long-legged grace.

"I got word your flight was delayed on the ground by bad weather in Atlanta." She reached for his bulging leather briefcase. "Did you have a rough trip?"

"I've had better," he drawled, his free hand closing over her wrist.

Startled, she jerked her head up. Her eyes were

brown, he noted dispassionately, a honey-dipped brown that reminded him of sweet, slow-pouring molasses.

"Care to tell me why you want to know?"

Those golden-brown eyes widened, then sparked with indignation. She jerked her wrist free.

"I don't want to know, particularly," she retorted. "I was just making small talk."

She must have seen the suspicion in his face. The hand he'd just captured made an impatient circle in the air.

"Look, I don't get paid extra for conversation with my pickups. If you want to dispense with the polite chit-chat, that's fine by me."

She was good, Jack thought. Very good. No beating about the bush. No coy, suggestive hints. She must have heard that those kinds of games hadn't worked the last time.

The stunning blonde who'd struck up a conversation with him during a financial administrators' conference in Tampa last month had tried a more indirect approach. Their meeting at the hotel bar after a long day of seminars and vendor displays had been casual, seemingly accidental, although the kind of entertainment she'd offered him in a throaty whisper was anything but.

Amused, Jack had declined her whiskey-voiced invitation to her room. Even if he'd had the time or the inclination, he preferred to choose his own companions. She'd pouted in pretty indignation, and her suggestions for ways to spend the rest of the evening had progressed from seductive to just this side of physically impossible. When Jack got up to leave, she'd scribbled her room number on a cocktail napkin and slipped it in his pocket—in case he changed his mind.

He'd understood her persistence when he walked

back into the bar to sign the tab he'd forgotten. The blonde had been huddled in a dark booth with a representative of a major drug distributing company...the same company that Jack's audits had hit particularly hard.

Their subtle attempt to buy him off with invitations to "conferences" in Aruba and Switzerland had failed. Obviously, they'd decided to try a different approach. Jack suspected that if he'd taken the woman up on her offer, embarrassing videotapes would have been delivered to his home, if not to his boss, soon after his return from Tampa.

The ploy hadn't worked then. It wouldn't work now.

Although...

Jack had to admit that the idea of attempting a few of those energetic, impossible acts with this doe-eyed woman held far more appeal than they had when suggested by the blonde.

He'd been working *way* too hard, he decided. That was the only explanation he could come up with for his inexplicable attraction to the woman eyeing him with something less than cordiality right now. Her expression about twenty degrees colder than the surprisingly mild air, she walked back to the dark blue sedan and pulled open the rear passenger door.

"Whenever you're ready."

Jack took in her square-shouldered stance and the exaggerated civility in her voice. Belatedly he realized that her elegant military-style tunic and slim skirt were more than just a fashion statement. She was here to pick him up, all right, but not necessarily in the manner he'd first assumed.

She must be the driver Gulliver's Travels had offered to provide, despite his instructions to the contrary. Annoyed, and feeling more than a little foolish, Jack crossed the walkway.

"I apologize if I sounded a bit brusque. It *was* a rough flight, and I wasn't expecting anyone to meet me."

She eyed him coolly. "Is that why you acted as though I was trying to steal your briefcase?"

"The possibility did cross my mind."

Among others.

"We've established my identity," he said, extending his hand. "And you are...?"

She hesitated, then took his hand. Her skin was warm and smooth, her grip surprisingly firm.

"Angela. Angela Paretti."

Jack turned the name over in his mind. It struck a familiar chord, but not one he could identify. He hadn't met her before. That much he was sure of. He would have remembered that generous mouth and spill of glossy hair.

"I'm Senator Claiborne's driver," she amplified, slipping her hand free of his. "We called your office this morning to notify you that I'd be waiting outside the Delta terminal. Obviously, you didn't get the word."

"No, I didn't," Jack replied, his annoyance spiking sharply. Claiborne's name, at least, he recognized immediately. "I didn't have time to check in with my office before my flight left."

Damn! He should have expected the senator to pull something like this. A throwback to the days of good-ol'-boy deals made in smoke-filled corridors, Senator Henry "Coon Dog" Claiborne had represented South Carolina in the nation's capital for more than four decades now. Crafty and immensely powerful, he chaired the subcommittee that had started looking into medical reform legislation long before it became a political buzzword. In his role as chairman of that subcommittee, he'd summoned Jack to Washington to discuss the audit program he'd instituted at Atlanta's Children's Hospital.

Jack had tried to avoid, or at least postpone, this trip. His data was too raw, he'd protested. The implications were too far-reaching to present without careful analysis and review. Senator Claiborne wouldn't be put off, however. As he'd phrased it, this would be a friendly little hearin'. There wasn't any need for congressional subpoenas between two "Suthrun gentlemen," but he surely would like to hear more about these audits, the ones causin' such a stir in the medical community.

With that call, the tightrope Jack had been walking for the past several months had stretched nearly to the breaking point. Apparently, the wily legislator had recognized that fact and sent his car and driver to make sure his reluctant witness made it to his "friendly little" prehearing appointments.

As if confirming his guess, the driver glanced pointedly at her watch. "I'm sorry about the mix-up, but it's a good thing the senator sent me to pick you up. With the delay in your flight, you wouldn't have had time to check out the rental car your office had reserved and still make your appointment with him. We'll barely make it as it is." She gestured gracefully toward the open rear door. "The senator doesn't like to be kept waiting."

Jack tamped down his irritation. It wasn't this woman's fault that her boss was a world-class manipulator. Tossing his gear onto the back seat, he slammed the door.

"I'll sit up front."

She shrugged. "Suit yourself. Let me just throw my stuff in the back."

"I've got it."

Her stuff, Jack discovered, included a black leather shoulder bag that weighed more than his carryall, an equally heavy textbook on United States political history, and a crumpled paper bag that gave off a mouthwatering aroma.

Pastries, he guessed. Freshly baked ones at that.

The scent of vanilla and yeasty dough set off a faint rumbling in his stomach. He hadn't had time to eat *or* call his office this morning, and it was now well past noon. Setting the bag beside the textbook in the back, he folded his tall frame into the passenger seat.

With the long, bumpy flight and this mix-up over transportation, his trip had gotten off to an uneven start. After his meeting with Senator Claiborne, Jack suspected matters would go from uneven to downright uncomfortable all around. He might as well relax and enjoy the short drive into the city with the senator's intriguing driver.

Angela walked around the rear of the dark blue Chrysler, shaking her head at her own carelessness. She'd almost missed him! After waiting for more than an hour for the senator's latest quarry to appear, she'd been standing there like an idiot, with her eyes closed and her face lifted to the sun. Of course, he'd chosen that particular moment to walk out of the terminal.

Thank goodness he'd paused on the walkway and she'd opened her eyes to find him staring at her. Her first response had been instinctive—a tiny dart of pleasure any woman might feel at the unmistakable interest of an attractive man. Her pleasure had evaporated the moment she recognized him, though. She knew too much about Jack Merritt and his kind to feel flattered by his obvious interest.

Slipping into the driver's seat, she inserted the key into the ignition. With one ear tuned to the muted growl of the engine, Angela pulled on her seat belt, then waited while her passenger adjusted his to fit.

It took some adjusting. He was a big man. The grainy black-and-white picture one of the staffers had clipped from some obscure medical journal hadn't captured his size...or the intelligence in those gunmetal-gray eyes.

He didn't look like a medical bean counter, Angela decided with a quick, assessing glance. Not like the representatives of that particular subspecies that she'd dealt with in recent years, anyway. None of them had sported a thatch of jet-black hair with just a hint of a curl in its conservative cut, a square, uncompromising chin and shoulders a yard wide.

He had the uniform down pat, though, right down to the discreet, conservative stripe in his charcoal-gray suit. And the icy expression.

After that quick grin when she opened her eyes and caught him staring at her, he'd gone all cold and distant. Become downright unfriendly, in fact. Angela had shrugged off enough hostile looks from accountants and bill collectors in the past few years to have become immune to them. For some reason, though, this man's had bothered her. So much so that she'd lost her professional cool for a moment and snapped back at him.

Oh, well, it wasn't the first time she'd tossed out a smart rejoinder, and it probably wouldn't be the last. As Senator Claiborne was so fond of saying, he surely to goodness hadn't hired her for her diplomatic skills.

Pulling her gaze from her passenger, Angela punched a speed-dial button on the phone mounted within easy reach on the dash. One of the high school interns spending an eye-popping week in the hallowed halls of power answered on the first ring.

"Senator Claiborne's office."

"This is Angela. I've got Dr. Merritt, and we're on our way."

"Yes, ma'am."

Smiling at the teen's reedy voice, Angela pressed the end button.

"All set?" she inquired of her passenger.

"All set."

Wrapping her hands around the wheel, she checked the side and rearview mirrors, then peeled away from the curb. As always, the responsiveness of the specially modified engine sent a tiny thrill through her veins. With the precision of a surgeon, she cut across two lanes and sliced a place for the Chrysler in the bumper-to-bumper traffic.

A jerk of the wool-covered knee next to hers drew her attention. Amused, she saw two rather large feet shod in black Córdoba leather had planted themselves against the plush floor mats. Hard.

Hiding a smile, Angela settled into the short, familiar run along Memorial Parkway. Winter-bare Virginia countryside rolled by on the left. Sunlight sparkled on the silvery-gray waters of the Potomac on the right. She'd made this run too many times to count, and she always enjoyed the uncluttered beauty of this brief stretch of parkway. This time, she barely noticed it. The man beside her absorbed her full attention.

Although her initial attempt at polite conversation had met with something less than notable success, professional courtesy demanded that she give it another shot.

"Is this your first visit to Washington, Dr. Merritt?"

"The first in a long time," he replied, with the faint drawl that was a mere echo of the one her boss could lay on when he wanted to. "And it's Jack."

"I beg your pardon?"

"Call me Jack. We do things more informally where I come from—and more slowly!"

His arm shot out to brace against the dash as a van cut in scant yards ahead of them. With smooth skill, Angela swung the heavy Chrysler around the other vehicle.

"Don't worry, Dr. Merritt...Jack. I haven't lost a passenger yet."

His arm dropped. "That's good to hear."

"Of course," she mused, "there's a first time for everything."

He didn't reply to that deliberately provocative remark, but his dark brows winged upward when a speed-limit sign whizzed by a few seconds later. Angela caught his pained expression, and the irrepressible Paretti grin that was never far from the surface pulled at her mouth.

"All right. I admit it. I like to run with the lead pack."

"So I noticed."

His drawl was more noticeable this time, almost as down-home as the senator's, but...sexier. She shrugged off its rippling effect on her nerves. So the man had a voice like melted carmel. If she hadn't learned anything else in the past three years, she'd certainly learned that a pleasing appearance and a pleasant manner counted for little when money was on the line. Even barracudas could exude a certain charm while they ripped the flesh from your bones.

"Have you always had this predilection for speed?" he asked, keeping a cautious eye on the road. "Or is it an acquired taste?"

"It's in my blood. My brother Tony swears I'm even worse than he is when it comes to standing on the gas."

"Tony?"

She could tell the moment he made the connection. His head angled, and recognition flared in his eyes.

"Your brother is Tony Paretti, the race-car driver?"

"The former race-car driver." She kept her tone even. "He hasn't raced in a few years."

Three years and seven months, to be exact.

"I remember reading about his crash," her passenger said quietly.

Angela's nails dug into the leather-wrapped steering wheel. Even now, after all this time, the memory of that hot, horrifying July day when her brother's car had thrown a wheel and smoked into a wall could close her throat. Not even the long, agonizing weeks while he hovered between life and death and the Paretti family's world came crashing down around them had approached those few seconds of undiluted terror.

"I saw him on TV recently." Merritt's deep voice pulled her from the black, billowing smoke. "He was doing a commercial... No, a public-service spot in support of stricter enforcement of drunk-driving sanctions."

Angela forced a smile. "Sponsors would have him hawking everything from soapsuds to racing souvenirs if he'd let them, but Tony's careful what he lends his name to."

"Smart man."

"He is. Very smart."

She stared out the windshield, her eyes on the ribbon

of gray asphalt ahead, but her mind filled with the image of her laughing, teasing brother. Six years older, he'd been her idol since she was old enough to toddle after him. Tony had chuckled at her constant demands for his attention, and spoiled her rotten. Even in the close-knit, clannish community in Baltimore where they grew up, the Parettis had shared a special bond.

"He's still something of a hero on the NASCAR Winston Cup circuit." Pride, undiminished by time or circumstance, colored her words. "He was the first rookie in thirty years to win one of Daytona's twin qualifying races, you know."

"No, I didn't know."

She shot him a quick look. No, of course, he wouldn't know that bit of racing trivia. Jack Merritt wouldn't have more than a passing knowledge—if that!—of the fast, exhilarating, dangerous world she'd grown up in.

He was a product of another world, Angela reminded herself. A world that had almost ground her family into the dirt. He was a number cruncher, for heaven's sake. She'd had enough unpleasant experiences with his type to last her a lifetime.

Flipping on the directional signal, Angela cut into the exit lane. Moments later, the Chrysler made a smooth, pavement-hugging curve up the ramp to the Fourteenth Street Bridge.

"Have you been driving for Senator Claiborne long?" Merritt asked, breaking the small silence.

"Almost three years."

"I didn't realize members of Congress were assigned personal cars and drivers."

Her mouth curled in a small, sardonic smile. She should have known it wouldn't take long for the auditor to come out.

"They're not. Most drive themselves, or use the congressional motor pool."

"But not the senior senator from South Carolina?"

Angela could have told him that her boss's diminished vision made him something of a hazard on the road. That his staff secretly referred to him as E.T. because of all his close encounters. She could have admitted that Senator Clairborne had given her the job she so desperately needed as much for the safety of the general population as for his own convenience. But her loyalty to the senator went too deep for her to discuss him with anyone. Instead, she tossed Merritt's question back at him.

"Worried about your tax dollars?"

"Should I be?"

"Not in this instance. This car belongs to Senator Clairborne, not the U.S. government, and he pays my salary from his personal—"

"Watch out!"

She didn't need either his terse warning or the quick, reflexive stomp of his foot against the floor mat. She'd already seen the stalled traffic ahead and begun pumping the antilock brakes.

She wasn't the only driver hitting the brakes. All around them, the air filled with squeals of protest from steel-belted tires as six lanes of vehicles screeched and slowed. Scant seconds later, the Chrysler jerked to a stop, inches from the fender of the car ahead.

Merritt raked his black hair into place with one hand. "Nice stop."

Angela nodded absently, her eyes on the snarl of vehicles ahead. All six northbound lanes into the district had come to a complete standstill. As far as she could see, nothing was moving. Even by Washington standards, this kind of logjam was unusual.

"Great," she muttered, drumming her fingers on the wheel.

"Looks like the senator might have to wait a little longer."

The hint of satisfaction in Merritt's voice rubbed Angela the wrong way. Like UPS, she prided herself on delivering her boss and his visitors to their destinations on time, every time. Switching off the ignition, she yanked on the door handle.

"Sit tight. I'll go see what the problem is."

"I need to stretch my legs," he said, reaching into the back seat for his trench coat. "I'll go with you."

With a thin black sweater layered under her wool tunic, Angela didn't need to retrieve the coat she kept in the Chrysler's trunk. Still, the sun reflecting off the Potomac felt welcome as she moved to the front of the vehicle and stepped up on the bumper. She teetered for a moment, then stiffened when two large hands closed around her waist and steadied her. Startled at the steely strength of Merritt's hold, she forced herself not to jerk away.

Whatever had caused the tie-up must have occurred beyond the point where the traffic exited the bridge. All Angela could see ahead was long lines of stalled traffic. Twisting, she looked back the way they'd come. To her disgust, vehicles had already begun stacking up on the Virginia side of the river.

Wonderful! They couldn't go forward, and there certainly wasn't any going back.

As if to mock the stranded motorists, traffic still whizzed by, unimpeded, in the southbound lanes. Observing the free flow on the opposite bridge span, Angela muttered a short, pithy exclamation under her breath. She'd learned the phrase from Tony's pit crew as a youngster, but she hadn't said it aloud since the day her brother caught her using it to entertain her third grade classmates.

"We're going to be here a while," she told Merritt, stepping off the bumper. "A *long* while."

His hands fell away from her waist. To Angela's consternation, she noticed their absence almost as much as she had their presence.

"I've been stuck in worse places," he replied. "We might as well relax and enjoy the fresh air. Relatively fresh air," he amended, taking in a whiff of the fumes rising from the vehicles idling their engines in the futile expectation of moving anytime soon.

"You enjoy the fresh air. I'll go call the office."

She left him leaning against the front fender, surveying the columned beauty of the Jefferson Memorial, which loomed at the north end of the bridge. After explaining the situation to the intern, who promised to make sure the senator got the word, Angela debated what to do next.

She could leave Merritt outside by himself, gawking at the view like a tourist, she supposed. She wasn't under any obligation to entertain him during what looked to be a long, frustrating delay. More to the point, she didn't have any desire to entertain him. He represented a system she'd come to despise.

She waited for the spurt of contempt that generally accompanied any reminder of a bureaucratic process that put money ahead of people. It arrived, but with something less than its usual force.

Was Tony right? she wondered, her brow furrowing. Was it time to put the accident and its aftermath behind

her? Maybe she shouldn't have become so deeply involved in the senator's determined efforts to reform the
health care system. Shouldn't have looked forward so
eagerly to this witness's public grilling.

Well, it was too late now for doubts and second
thoughts. Like a sacrificial goat, Jack Merritt would be
offered up on the altar of medical reform in less than
forty-eight hours.

Her fingers beating a jerky tattoo, Angela studied the
man through the windshield. Despite her determination
to view him only as a necessary means to an end, she
found that she wanted to know more about him than
what she'd learned in the sketchy bio the staff had put
together. Wanted to take the measure of the man the
senator intended to put on the rack.

Even sacrificial goats deserved a last meal, she decided abruptly. Reaching behind her, she retrieved the
white paper bag from the back seat. Then she grabbed
a wad of tissues from her purse and joined Merritt at
the side of the car.

"Are you hungry?"

His gaze flicked over her face, then caught on the
paper sack. Something very much like amusement
flared his eyes for a moment.

"As a matter of fact, I am. I've been sneaking whiffs
of whatever's in that bag since I got in the car."

"What's in this bag," she announced, "is pure art-
istry, courtesy of my aunt Helen. She sends a care package with my cousin Leonard whenever he drives into
the city."

Perching on the fender, she rolled down the neck of
the sack and held it out for Merritt's inspection.

"You have a choice. The best homemade cannoli this

side of the Atlantic, or heart-shaped tortoni cookies, in honor of the occasion.''

"What occasion?"

"You're kidding, right?"

When she saw that he wasn't, she lifted a leg and waggled her foot. The sequined hearts on her sneakers sparkled in the sun like miniature stoplights.

"Today is Valentine's Day. Why else would I be wearing these?"

"I wondered," he murmured.

This time, the amusement was clear, and altogether too potent for Angela's peace of mind. Disconcerted, she rattled the paper bag.

"Which do you want?"

"I'll try a cannoli."

Using a tissue, she handed a flaky deep-fat-fried pastry stuffed with ricotta and sinfully rich whipped cream to Merritt.

She'd just claimed another for herself when the first shot rang out.

# *Chapter 2*

Angela knew instantly that the whiplike crack wasn't the sound of a car backfiring. She could identify an engine in every one of its voices, and that wasn't one of them. Street-smart and Trained by experts for every contingency a professional driver might face, she suspected what had caused the sharp report even before she threw a quick, instinctive look over her shoulder.

A steady of stream of vehicles rumbled by in the southbound lanes. Angela swept them with a lightning-like glance. At first she didn't see anything to alarm her. Then, in one of those nightmarish half seconds that seem to last a lifetime, she caught a glimpse of a pale face peering from an open car window. Just below the white blur, a few inches of blue-black barrel protruded through the open window.

"Oh, my God!"

Her heart and her lungs and her fists all squeezed shut. The pastry in her hand disintegrated into mush.

With whipped cream flying in all directions, she launched herself off the fender and hit Merritt squarely in the chest. He staggered back, taking her with him.

"What the—?"

"Get down!"

She buckled her knees and dropped like a bag of stones in his arms. She didn't know whether it was her dead weight or Merritt's recognition of the danger that did the trick, but suddenly his body came crashing down atop hers. What little air was left in her lungs departed with a *whump*.

The same instant her face pressed into the pavement, another crack split the air. The Chrysler's rear passenger windows exploded. Razor-edged shards of safety glass rained down all around them. A startled shout came from just behind their vehicle. A woman screamed.

Squeezing her eyes shut, Angela buried her face in goo-filled palms. She couldn't move. Couldn't breathe. Didn't try to do either. Her blood roared in her ears, so loudly she barely heard the third, then fourth, pop that signaled that the shooter was speeding south.

As quickly as it had erupted, the violence ended. All that remained was a chorus of shouts and screams coming from somewhere behind them, and Merritt's rock-solid weight pinning her to the pavement. Angela felt his breath, hot and fast, on her cheek. One of his knees dug into the back of her calf.

She burrowed under his protective shield for several long seconds before her starved lungs demanded air. Squirming, she tried to shift his bulk.

At her movement, Merritt levered himself off her prone body. Sucking in quick, relieved breaths, Angela wedged herself up on one elbow and shoved her hair out of her eyes. She expected to find the face so close to hers tight with shock or anger. Even fear. The Lord knew her heart was still thundering in her chest!

If Jack Merritt felt any of those emotions, however, he didn't show them. Much. Only the pulsing tic on one side of his jaw and the razor-sharp edge to his voice betrayed his inner state.

"Are you all right?" He rapped out the question.

"I...I think so. You?"

"I'm okay."

When he started to rise, Angela grabbed at his arm and gasped out a warning.

"Careful! You've got glass in your hair."

Leaning away from her, he shook his head. The movement dislodged a small shower of silvery shards. They hit the pavement with a joyful tinkle that sounded obscene in the circumstances. Then he eased himself up on one knee and curled a hand under her arm to help her.

Wary of the broken glass, Angela got to her feet. For a few seconds, she experienced the oddest sense of disorientation. The February sun still sparkled on the Potomac. Cars still whizzed by on the opposite bridge span. In the distance, gulls swooped and chattered above the Tidal Basin.

Yet the narrow slice of world contained on the northbound span had spilled into chaos. Car doors slammed all along the rows of stalled traffic. People poured out of their vehicles, shouting, exclaiming, assuring each other that they weren't hurt. A baby screeched in the arms of a hysterical mother. An army officer stood beside a black sports car, staring in disbelief at a starburst in the windshield. Some distance behind him, two women were waving and pointing at what Angela guessed was a bullet hole in the rear fender of their car.

She didn't need to see a hole to know what had just happened. She had ample proof close at hand. Both of the Chrysler's rear windows were shattered. Jagged shards edged the chrome frame of the window closest to her, looking much like shark's teeth in a gaping maw.

She clenched her fists, unmindful of the whipped cream that squished through her fingers. Anger seared through her, hot and scorching.

She wasn't naive. She knew that mindless violence could spark anywhere, at any time, over something as trivial as a kid's jacket or a wrong turn down a one-way street. She also understood danger. She'd spent summers and weekends at racetracks where men pushed the limits of machines, and death was only a heartbeat away. Her soul splintering, she'd watched sheets of flame engulf her brother's car.

She accepted risk. Understood that danger was a part of life. Yet, somehow, she wasn't prepared for the raw fury this wanton, random act generated. Her whole body quivered with the force of it.

"Here, put this on."

She flung her head up and caught the sharp concern in her passenger's face as he draped his trench coat around her shoulders.

"I'm not cold!"

"You're shaking," he said tersely. "You could be going into shock."

"What I'm going into is total, one hundred percent—" she searched the air with her hands for a word to describe her feelings "—outrage! Look what they did!"

Her anger boiled over as she surveyed her wounded car.

"I've read about people getting caught in drive-by

shootings," she ground out through clenched teeth. "But until something like that happens to you, you never realize how…how furious it makes you!"

"Is that what you think happened? A drive-by shooting?"

Her head snapped up. "Of course! What else?"

Jack wasn't ready to answer that one. Not when his pulse was still pounding and cold sweat was drying on the back of his neck.

"I don't know."

She dismissed his disclaimer with a short, choppy wave. Spinning on her heel, she crunched through the glass. "I'm going to call 911."

While she made the call, Jack stared at the shattered windows. His logical, orderly mind tried to accept the idea of random violence, to anchor it in reality by calculating the probability factor.

What were the odds of a trigger-happy goon or hopped-up gang member driving by this particular spot at this particular time and deciding to take potshots at stalled traffic? What were the chances that he and Angela Paretti would be among the stranded motorists? One in a million? One in ten million? Grimly, Jack decided that there were too many variables involved for him to work the equation right now. And too many unknowns.

Like why six lanes of traffic had come to a screeching halt.

And why the Chrysler seemed to have taken most of the hits.

And why the senator had sent Angela Paretti to meet him at the airport in the first place.

His gaze sliced to the woman standing a few feet away, her face smeared with cream and her slender frame enveloped in his trench coat. Her free hand punctuated the air as she described the shooting to the police dispatcher. Listening to her account, Jack replayed the sequence of events in his mind.

Once again, he heard the sharp, distinctive report of a high-powered rifle. Saw the dark cloud of Angela's hair as she whipped her head around. Felt the impact of her body as she threw herself against him.

His jaw locked. Whatever the variables, whatever the unknowns, there was one absolute in the equation. Angela had pulled him down, out of harm's way. Jack owed her for that, and he was a man who believed in balancing his debits and credits.

Shoving his balled fists into his pants pockets, he waited while she finished the call and made another, lengthier one to her office. She replaced the phone on its mount a few moments later, grimacing at the smears she left on its casing. With a muttered exclamation, she dug into a side pocket in the door and pulled out a tissue. A few swipes got rid of most of the cream.

"The senator's on the floor for a roll-call vote," she told Jack tersely, the tissue shredding as she scrubbed at her hands. "His aide promised to get word to him right away."

"Looks like our meeting will have to wait a while longer."

Her forehead folded into the beginnings of a frown that got sidetracked into another grimace. Wadding the tissue, she dabbed at her temple.

"Yech! I've got cream all over my face. I feel it, even if I can't see it."

"I can." He reached into his suit coat and pulled out a folded handkerchief. "Here, I'll get it."

She hesitated, then tipped her chin to his waiting hands.

This was how he'd first seen her, Jack thought as he curled one hand around her chin and cleaned the cream from her forehead and cheeks. With her face to the sun and her hair spilling down her back. A small shock rippled through him when he realized he'd caught his first glimpse of Angela Paretti less than twenty minutes ago.

It seemed longer. A lot longer. As though it had occurred in a different life. Somehow, a few seconds of shared danger had divided time into two halves. Before the shots, and after. Before Angela had thrown herself into his arms, and after. Before a bond had been forged between him and this woman, and after.

He studied her face while he worked, pondering the new set of unknowns that suddenly engaged his mind. Like the complexity of a woman who quivered with barely suppressed fury over an incident like this, instead of shaking with shock or fear. And the feel of her warm flesh beneath his fingertips. And his sudden desire to lick away the dollop of cream decorating her left earlobe.

"You're pretty calm," she mumbled, "considering that someone was taking potshots at us a few minutes ago."

"I don't like it any more than you did."

"You don't show it."

"I don't show a lot of things."

She gave a huff of derision. "Do they teach you that in Accounting I? Never show any emotion, or your clients might make the mistake of thinking you're human?"

Jack paused in his self-appointed task. "Have you dealt with a lot of accountants, human or otherwise?"

"I've dealt with a few," she shot back.

"Some of us experience a basic emotion or two on occasion."

"Ha! That I'd have to see to believe."

He couldn't have resisted the challenge if he wanted to, which he didn't. Intellectually he understood that she was just venting the simmering emotion spawned by the shooting. He also understood that there was more to her apparent aversion to members of his profession than he grasped at this moment. But for all his rigid control, for all his rational explanation of her anger, Jack's blood still pounded through his veins. And her mouth was too close to his.

"Then keep your eyes open, Angela."

He lowered his head slowly, deliberately, giving her time to pull away. Her face registered a startled surprise that quickly escalated into a glower, but she stood her ground. Satisfaction arrowed through him at her stubborn refusal to give an inch. Then he covered her mouth with his, and satisfaction vaulted into hunger.

He tasted whipped cream and warm flesh and woman. No, not just woman. *This* woman. She had a flavor all her own, one that came through the traces of vanilla and cream clinging to her lips. Jack's senses recorded her taste, her scent, her feel, and demanded more. His hand slid from her chin to her throat. His other hand curled into a fist to keep from burying his fingers in her hair and tipping her head back to explore the dark, satiny depths of her mouth.

That would come. Later. He hoped.

When he lifted his head, he was breathing as hard and fast as she was. Hiding a smile at the emotions chasing across her expressive face, he stepped back and waited for the explosion.

Angela wasn't sure what shocked her more. The fact that Jack Merritt had kissed her, or that she'd let him.

He was the goat, for heaven's sake! The senator's next victim in his crusade to reform health care. More to the point, he was the walking, talking personification of a system that had almost ground her family into the dust!

She couldn't believe she'd just stood here, heart hammering and eyes open as he'd instructed, and let him kiss her! Or that the mere touch of his mouth on hers could ignite sparks hotter and faster than the power combustion-control unit Tony had installed in his Monte Carlo the week before he won at Daytona.

It was the violence that had held her motionless, she decided breathlessly. The anger that still sizzled her nerves and fueled her emotions. Not the way his broad shoulders blocked everything from her view. Or the warmth of his hand on her chin. Or the scent of fine wool and tangy after-shave that enveloped her.

She dragged in a swift, sharp breath. "If that little demonstration was supposed to prove something, you missed the mark. Big-time."

"Did I? Maybe I should try again."

Her eyes flashed a warning. "Maybe you shouldn't. In fact, maybe you should just—"

The distant wail of sirens stopped her just in time. With a look that let her passenger know he'd been saved by the bell, she yanked his coat from around her shoulders.

"Thanks for the loan," she said acidly.

"Any time."

Folding her arms, Angela propped her hips against

the front fender and tried to shift her pulse back into low gear. It wasn't easy, with Merritt leaning against the same fender, his thigh too close to hers.

The squads of officers who converged on the scene worked their way methodically through the maze of stalled vehicles and excited motorists. Finally, a uniformed D.C. police officer approached the Chrysler.

Short and stubby, she wore a Sam Browne belt around her waist and a bulky, bulletproof vest under her blue uniform shirt and jacket. A metal nameplate identified her as L. Hemmingway. Surveying the broken windows and shards of glass on the pavement, she flipped to a clean page in her notebook and addressed Merritt—the obvious authority figure, Angela thought with a stab of impatience.

"We've had reports of shots fired from a passing vehicle. Is that what caused the damage to this car?"

"That's what it looks like."

"Did you see the car the shots came from?"

"No, I didn't."

She turned to Angela, her expression polite but evincing little expectation of success. "How about you, ma'am? Did you see a vehicle that might have—"

"I saw it."

"You did?" Cautious hope flared on the officer's face. "Can you describe it? The color? Whether it had two or four doors?"

Angela prayed for patience. She was used to dealing with men who considered females complete airheads when it came to anything and everything on wheels, but she expected better from another woman.

"It was a '93 Pontiac Grand Prix," she stated flatly. "Metallic gray, with red pinstriping on the front fenders and oversize Michelin tires on the rear axle that elevated it into what the kids on the street call a California rake. I couldn't see the plates, but from the smoke trail that sucker was laying down, I *could* see that it needed a ring job. Badly.''

The officer gaped at her. ''Are you sure about these details, Ms.—?''

''Paretti. Angela Paretti. And I'm sure.''

''Paretti,'' the officer mumbled, scribbling down the name. When she looked up again, a layer of official courtesy almost covered her skepticism. ''The suspect vehicle had to be moving pretty fast. How did you happen to catch so much detail?''

Angela gave her a pitying look. ''If I could learn to read my brother's hand signals as he drove by the pit at a hundred and ninety miles an hour, I could hardly miss the details of a Grand Prix slugging along at fifty or sixty.''

''Your brother drove by at a hundred and ninety miles an hour?'' Hemmingway gasped as enlightenment dawned. ''Hey, is your brother Tony Paretti?''

''Yes.''

''I saw him on TV a couple of weeks ago.'' A dreamy expression drifted across the pudgy officer's face for a second or two. Then she recalled herself with a little shake. ''Okay, so let me get this down. You saw the car—''

''And the shooter.''

Hemmingway's pencil skittered. Excitement lit her pale blue eyes. ''You saw the shooter? Can you describe him?''

Angela summoned a mental image. ''He was a Caucasian male, late teens or early twenties, I'd guess. He had a thin, kind of longish face. Oh, and he was wearing a sweater or a sweatshirt in sort of a putrid green.''

"Green!" Disgust flitted across the officer's plump face. "That sounds like the Horsemen. Those punks wear a green jacket. This could've been one of their damned initiation rites."

She jotted down the details in her notebook, then flipped it shut. "It sounds like you got a pretty good look at him, good enough to describe him to a composite artist. I'll have to ask you to come with me, ma'am."

"Now?"

"Now. It's important that you work with an artist while the details are still fresh in your mind. I'll call ahead and have one of the computer composite techs waiting at our district headquarters."

"Can't we delay that for an hour or so?" Angela protested. "Dr. Merritt has an appointment with Senator Claiborne. I need to get him there as soon as this logjam clears."

At the mention of the senator's name, Hemmingway's ruddy complexion paled. Crunching through the broken glass, she peered at the Chrysler's license plate. When she spotted the metal congressional emblem in one corner, she gave a low groan.

"Oh, no! This is Coon Dog Claiborne's car? The mayor's not going to like this."

Angela understood the officer's dismay. Henry Claiborne had voiced his dissatisfaction on more than one occasion with the crime plaguing the nation's capital. And when one of his constituents was mugged within shouting distance of the Russell Building, the outraged legislator had zinged off a scorching letter that made the front page of the *Washington Post*.

Since the senator also happened to chair the committee that appropriated funds for D.C.'s annual operating budget each year, the mayor had hastily put together a sweeping anticrime program. Not quite sweeping enough, evidently.

L. Hemmingway settled her holster on her hips with a nervous twitch. "I'm afraid I have to insist that you come with me, Ms. Paretti. We need you to do that composite and, uh, talk to the detective who'll work this case. We'll get Dr...."

"Merritt."

"...Dr. Merritt to his appointment."

"I'll go with you and Ms. Paretti."

The officer turned to face him, her polite mask firmly in place. "That's not necessary, sir. Since you didn't see anything, we don't need to detain you...or, uh, keep the senator waiting."

"I might not have seen the vehicle, but I did hear the shots."

"We've got sufficient confirmation of the shots, and we're searching for expended bullets that might give us a clue as to the type of weapon used. Now, if you'll just—"

"It was a single-round semiautomatic Assault Kalashnikov, more commonly known as an AK."

This time, both the police officer and Angela gaped.

"The AK-47 has a distinctive sound," Merritt said calmly. "Easily identifiable to anyone who's heard it before."

Hemmingway recovered first. She scribbled furiously in her notebook, then stuffed it in her jacket pocket.

"Why don't you give me the keys to the senator's vehicle, Ms. Paretti? I'll arrange to have it towed to district headquarters when traffic starts moving. In the meantime, I'd like you both to come with me."

Angela sighed in resignation. "All right. But let me

call the office first and tell them we'll be delayed. Again.''

Moments later, she buckled herself into the back seat of a black-and-white police cruiser beside Merritt. The door slammed shut, the automatic locks clicked loudly. As she surveyed the thick plastic screen inset with wire mesh that separated the back seat from the front, the hair on the back of her neck prickled. She felt as though she were caught in a cage with Merritt.

A small cage.

He was so close. Too close. With just a slight angle of her head, she could see the fine lines webbing the corners of his gray eyes. The rebellious wave in his black hair that was almost tamed by his no-nonsense cut. The glitter of a tiny shard buried in the collar of his charcoal suit coat.

"You've got a piece of glass in your collar. Hold still.''

She plucked it free, then looked for somewhere to discard it. Since the cruiser didn't appear to come equipped with ashtrays, she dug a wad of sticky tissue from her tunic pocket, wrapped up the sliver of glass and tucked it back in her pocket.

"Thanks.''

She nodded, waiting until the cruiser had turned and headed into the District before asking the question that hovered in her mind.

"I wonder how many people can identify an AK-47 just by its sound?''

"Probably about the same percentage of the population who can tell a '93 Grand Prix needs a ring job by observing its exhaust plume.'' He gave her an admiring smile. "I was as impressed as Officer Hemmingway, by the way.''

She refused to let either his compliment or his smile distract her. "How do you know so much about guns?"

"I did a tour in the navy."

"I thought sailors, you know—" she sketched some waves in the air "—swabbed decks and peered through periscopes."

"Some do," he said easily, then nodded to a huge granite building on the right. "Is that the old post office building? I haven't seen it since it was renovated."

Angela frowned at what she suspected was a deliberate turn in the conversation, but murmured an appropriate response. For the rest of the short trip to police headquarters, she struggled with the uneasy feeling that Jack Merritt wasn't quite fitting into his goatskin the way he was supposed to.

# Chapter 3

Second District headquarters buzzed with activity. Phones shrilled, keyboards clattered, and a steady stream of uniformed officers, handcuffed suspects, complainants and unidentified persons passed by the waiting area.

Jack had no difficulty schooling himself to patience while he waited for the detective who'd been assigned to the shooting. Propping the back edge of the plastic chair against the wall, he folded his arms and allowed himself the pleasure of watching Angela Paretti pace the waiting room. Her glittery sneakers flashed a bright counterpoint to the scuffed tan tile floor and nondescript furniture as she covered the room in a graceful stride that was enough to make any man sit up and take notice.

Any man.

He speared the derelict across the room with a quick frown. The bag man ignored his pointed glance and leered at Angela like a shaggy, unkempt wolf contemplating a stray lamb. Jack had just decided to put himself between Angela and the seedy character when a lean, wiry black man in a rumpled blue shirt and a shoulder holster strolled down the hall.

"Angie? What the hell are you doing setting yourself up for target practice, girl?"

She turned, a grin spreading across her face. "Hi, Eddie. I was afraid I'd get stuck with you."

The detective chuckled. "Hey, at least we're on the same side this time. How's Uncle Guido doing, anyway?"

"He's retired. For good!"

"Oh, yeah? Then how come we got a report that he was at the Mint again last week?"

"He was just feeling nostalgic. Honest. He said he only wanted to watch the hundred-dollar bills rolling off the press."

The detective snorted. "Yeah, right! I'm telling you, Angie, I better not see a rise in reports of counterfeit C-notes floating around the city in the next few weeks."

"You won't. Trust me, Eddie. Everything's under control."

Listening to the exchange, Jack added another variable to the complex equation that was Angela Paretti. The woman certainly seemed to live in a world populated by distinctive personalities. Her legendary boss. Her famous brother. Now, apparently, Uncle Guido, the retired counterfeiter.

"Dr. Merritt?" The detective approached, his hand extended. "I'm Ed Winters. I'd like to go over the statements you and Angie gave Officer Hemmingway, then we'll get her working on a composite. My office is just down the hall."

Slinging her black leather purse over one shoulder,

Angela led the way. Obviously, she'd been to Detective Winters's office before. Jack hefted the briefcase he'd retrieved from the Chrysler and followed.

The Second District detectives shared a large, noisy room at the back of the station. Taking one of the plastic chairs in front of a cluttered desk, Angela declined Winters's offer of coffee. When Jack did the same, the detective picked up a single typed sheet, then hitched a hip on the corner of his desk.

"We're still running the metallic-gray Grand Prix through the computers. Anything you can add to the details you gave Hemmingway, Angie?"

"Not really. The whole thing happened so fast. I saw the car and the gun barrel and the face all in the same instant. I probably wouldn't have noticed the Pontiac at all if it hadn't been laying down a trail of smoke."

"Yeah, bad valves."

"Bad rings, Eddie. Bad rings. There *is* a difference, you know."

"I'll take your word for it."

When she shook her head in mock disgust, he grinned and shifted his attention to Jack.

"Let's talk about the weapon. Why do you think the shots were fired from an AK-47?"

"It has a distinct report. Louder and a little sharper than the U.S.-made semiautomatics."

"And you've heard that distinctive sound before?"

He gave Winters the same answer he'd given Angela. "I served a hitch in the navy."

"The navy, huh?"

"The SEALs."

"Infiltration and extraction or covert ops?"

Jack shot him a swift look.

"I spent a few years in ~~military~~ intelligence," Win-

ters said with a shrug. "I know, I know, a lot of folks
think that's a contradiction in terms, but I did manage
to learn a thing or two about roles and missions."

Faced with the detective's obvious knowledge, Jack
reopened a chapter in his life that he'd closed a long
time ago.

"I was the hospital corpsman on an infiltration and
extraction team. I just went along for the ride, to patch
up whoever needed it."

Winters's expression indicated that he knew damn
well a navy SEAL team didn't take anyone along for
the ride.

"Now you're chief moneyman for—" he scanned the
typed report in his hand "—Children's Hospital in Atlanta. Interesting career change."

"Treating wounds on the run isn't exactly the kind
of thing a man makes a career out of. After the navy, I
went back to school and ended up in the business end
of medicine."

"I see. Well, I appreciate the information you've
given us. Wish I could tell you that AKs are rare around
these parts, or that we'll be able to track down the
weapon used in this incident. Unfortunately, the street
punks here are as partial to rapid-fire weapons as I suspect the gangs in Atlanta are."

"We've treated a few gang members at Children's,"
Jack admitted quietly. "The last one was seven years
old."

"Yeah." The detective dropped the report on the
desk and rose. "Sorry your visit to our fair city got off
to such an eventful start."

Jack's gaze shifted to the tousle-haired woman edg-
ing her way past him to the door. *Eventful* wasn't quite
how he'd describe it.

Winters snagged his suit jacket from the back of his chair. "I understand Angie was driving you to a meeting with Senator Claiborne. I'll get one of the uniforms to drive you to the Capitol Building while she works on the composite."

"I'll wait."

Angela jerked her head around.

"I brought my briefcase," Jack said calmly, forestalling her protest, "but I left my carryall in the car. There are some spreadsheets in it I want to review before my meeting with your boss."

"The senator is *not* going to be happy about this." With that ominous warning, Angela marched out the door.

Tough. Jack wasn't particularly happy about this summons to Washington, either. Until he understood exactly what was behind the senator's sudden "invitation," he intended to play this game slowly and very, very carefully. He didn't care if it took Angela the rest of the afternoon and half the night to complete the composite.

Unfortunately, she made short work of it. While he and Winters watched from the back of the room, she described the individual she'd glimpsed with words and the extravagant gestures Jack was coming to recognize as part of her vivid personality. A civilian technician seated at a computer console translated both words and gestures into a visual imaging program. Within moments, a face took form on the computer screen. With each click of the mouse, the form took on more distinct characteristics.

"Make the chin smaller." She butted the base of her palms together to demonstrate. "More pointed. Yes!

No! That's too much. Good. Now flatten out the cheeks. Ummmm...not that square. Okay, you got it.''

"Let's work on the nose next," the civilian tech suggested, clicking away. "Short?"

"Longer."

"Thin?"

"Thicker."

"Bulbous?"

"Well..."

"How about this one? I call it the perp's proboscis. It seems to fit a lot of our clients."

An elephantine trunk suddenly sprouted on the face on the screen, and Angela gave a sputter of laughter. "No, it wasn't quite that long or thick."

Correcting, agreeing, exclaiming, she and the tech worked together as though they'd always been a team.

"She's something else," Winters commented with a shake of his head.

Jack didn't have any argument with that observation.

"Have you known her long?" he asked the detective casually.

"Just since we busted her uncle a couple of years ago. Well, I guess he's more of a great-uncle. I was never quite sure of the exact relationship."

"The retired counterfeiter?"

Winters snorted. "He wasn't retired then. We suspect he put something close to two hundred thousand into circulation before we nailed him."

Jack gave a soundless whistle. "I'm surprised he's already back on the street."

The detective hesitated, his cop's instinctive discretion obviously at war with what Jack guessed was a matter of public record.

"Guido didn't do any jail time," Winters said after

a few moments. "He should have. He damn well should have. But our so-called expert couldn't tie the bills we'd pulled off the street to the press the feds found in his hideaway in Maryland."

The detective's dark eyes settled on the woman leaning over the console, her brown hair spilling over her shoulders.

"Angie was right there with him, through the entire mess. She bailed him out, swore at the hearing that the family hadn't seen a penny of any illegal income. She produced bank statements and a stack of unpaid medical bills that made the judge's eyes bulge."

His gaze on Angela, Winters didn't catch Jack's slight stiffening.

"The Parettis are old-country, know what I mean?" he continued. "Family business is family business, and nobody else's. She didn't like having to hang their personal linen out to dry in public, that was obvious. But her testimony convinced the judge that Guido didn't roll the presses to help with Tony's bills, which was the only motive we could establish."

"That was Guido's motive? To help pay the costs of Tony Paretti's medical care?"

"We think so. Tony's accident pretty well wiped the Parettis out. He's doing okay now with his string of automotive parts stores, but it was touch and go there for a while. His folks had to sell their home. Angela quit grad school and was working two jobs, and still the vultures were demanding—"

Winters broke off, his gaze sliding sideways. "Well, you know how those things go."

"Yes," Jack replied slowly, "I do."

That explained a lot of things, not the least of which was Angela Paretti's antipathy toward accountants.

Although he didn't know the specifics of her brother's injuries, Jack guessed Tony would have spent a week to ten days in ICU, minimum. After that, he would've required orthopedic and neuro specialists. Probably several weeks on a ward. Months in rehab.

From what Winters had let drop, it sounded as though Tony's medical insurance had contained one of those unobtrusive escape clauses governing hazardous occupations that no one ever noticed until it was too late. Assuming, of course, he *had* insurance at the time of his accident.

A familiar weight settled in Jack's chest. How many families had he worked with over the years who faced the same kind of crisis? The numbers clicked in his mind. Five years at Children's, eleven at other hospitals. A hundred families a year, at least. Sixteen hundred desperate wives or husbands or parents or adult children, reeling under the double shock of their loved ones' illnesses and the cost of their care.

Although his position description at Children's filled two typed pages, in Jack's view, his duties boiled down to one basic function—providing a balance between the needs of the patient and the fiscal requirements of the hospital. He took fierce pride in the fact that Children's had the highest charity-case ratio of any facility its size in the country. No child was ever refused treatment. No consulting physician was ever pressured not to admit a patient without medical insurance. Not on his watch.

Admittedly, that hadn't always been the case. When he took over the financial reins at Children's, the non-profit institution had been on the verge of going under due to fiscal mismanagement, excessive waste and outright fraud. He'd attacked all three, mismanagement being the easiest to rectify. The fight against waste was a continuing battle. Fraud...

He rubbed the back of his neck. Fraud was the reason he walked the dangerous tightrope he now did. It was also the reason he was in Washington, watching a dark-haired woman paint pictures in the air with her hands.

"I think that's him," Angela pronounced a few moments later.

The civilian tech sat back in his chair, his hands still for the first time. "You sure? Step back and take another look."

She joined Jack and Ed Winters at the back of the room. Worrying her lower lip with her teeth, she squinted at the screen.

"I don't know. Maybe the forehead—? No, that's him. I think."

Jack studied the face, searching for some physical characteristic that would suggest the young man who owned that face was capable of firing shots at stranded motorists. He didn't find it. The kid could have been any one of the twenty-year-olds who worked as aides and orderlies at Children's.

"We'll spread the composite around," Winters said. "Hustle some of those green-shirted punks who call themselves the Horsemen in to take a look at it. Maybe we'll get lucky and make a match. We'll call you if we do, Angie."

"Good enough," she said, slinging her purse over her shoulder. "Now I need you to point me in the direction of my car keys."

"They should be at the front desk. You want to call your mother before you go? You can use my office."

She winced. "No! Not now! It'll take me an hour to

calm her down when she hears about the shooting, and I don't want to keep the senator waiting any longer.''

The detective escorted them to the busy entrance lobby and retrieved the keys from the uniformed desk sergeant. He handed them to Angie, along with a pink slip.

''What's this?''

''A bill for replacement of the rear windows. The captain had one of the rookies run the car by a repair shop while you worked on the composite. He figured it was the least your helpful, friendly metropolitan police could do for one of our nation's elected officials.''

''He figured it might take some of the edge off the senator's righteous wrath, you mean,'' Angela retorted.

''Will it?''

''Not a chance.''

''That's what I told the captain,'' Winters said smugly.

She laughed and tossed the keys in the air. ''See you around, Eddie.''

''See you, Angie. Tell Uncle Guido I'm watching him.''

''Will do.''

Jack nodded a farewell to the detective and followed Angela outside. They stood on the steps for a moment, scanning the multistory parking garage across the street.

''I hope to heck the attendant knows where we're parked,'' she muttered. ''After all these delays, I don't want to spend another hour searching for the car.''

They discovered the midnight-blue sedan parked conveniently just inside the entrance. Angela fumbled with the keys, then stretched out her arm and clicked the remote. The door locks snicked loudly. She clicked again, and the engine turned over with a low growl.

"Remote-control ignition? That's handy," Jack commented.

"It is if you want to make tracks," she replied with a toss of her head. "And we do."

Twenty minutes later, Angela flashed her ID at the Capitol Building security checkpoint, then drove into the underground parking garage reserved for legislators and their senior staff. When she pulled into the choice slot situated right beside the elevator, she sat back with a sigh of relief.

She'd delivered—finally!—the man the senator had set his sights on. The one both she and her boss suspected could prove the existence of a raw, festering wound in a system that badly needed reform. Now all she had to do was sit back and watch the fireworks.

She pressed the concealed switch she'd installed along with the remote ignition system. The engine subsided into well-mannered silence. Beside her, her passenger calmly stuffed the papers he'd been studying back into a side pocket of his carryall.

"You can leave your coat and bag here," she told him, reaching for her purse. "We'll make sure that they get to your hotel with you."

He joined her outside the car and smoothed a hand down his tie. "I take it that means you won't be driving me to my hotel?"

"No, I won't." Her rubber soles squeaked on the slick pavement as she led the way to the elevator. "The senator has an engagement this evening. He's rearranged his schedule to accommodate our unexpected delay, but he can't miss this appointment."

"In that case," Merritt said quietly, joining her at the

polished brass door, "I'd better thank you now for dragging me down, out of the line of fire."

She leaned on the elevator button. "You're welcome."

"And for the cannoli."

"You're welcome again."

"And for the kiss."

Her startled glance flew up to his. The overhead floods cast his face in strong lines and angles. Angela couldn't miss the path his gaze traced to her lips.

"For that," she said with a touch of asperity, "you're not so welcome."

"Did you keep your eyes open?"

"I beg your pardon?"

"When we kissed. Did you keep your eyes open?"

"Yes. No." Her hand cut circles in the air. "Mostly. But I told you, whatever that kiss was supposed to prove, it missed its mark."

"Maybe we'd better try it with your eyes closed next time."

The calm rejoinder took Angela's breath away. She'd been right about Jack Merritt the first time, she thought in disgust. Despite his serious shoulders, his misty gray eyes, and a kiss that put him off the scale in the technique department, he was entirely too analytical about what had happened between them on the bridge. Too removed from the whirling emotions that had held her motionless. Like so many of his profession.

"There isn't going to be a next time," she said shortly.

He didn't appear convinced, but the elevator swished open at that moment. Shifting his briefcase to his left hand, he held the doors for her with a strong right forearm. She brushed past him and stabbed at the button for the second floor.

As the oak-paneled cubicle whirred upward, he gave her a slow smile, so similar to the one she'd seen on his face when she first opened her eyes at the airport that Angela's pulse jumped.

"You know," he said conversationally, "a major part of my job involves calculating returns on investments. We both invested something in those few moments on the bridge. Something I estimate will return substantial dividends."

"Don't hold your breath," Angela muttered.

His smile followed her out of the elevator.

## Chapter 4

As Jack accompanied his escort through the Capitol's vast, soaring rotunda, a familiar tension gathered at the base of his skull. Once more, the questions that had plagued him since the senator's phone call played and replayed in his mind.

What was behind this sudden invitation to testify before his subcommittee? Was the timing just coincidence? Or did Coon Dog Claiborne have a hidden agenda, one that went beyond his proposed legislation on medical reform?

Tightening his grip on his briefcase, Jack matched his stride to Angela's as she skirted a knot of gawking tourists and led the way to a broad marble staircase. Despite the tension, or perhaps because of it, he found himself absorbing her fluid grace and sure, confident movements with heightened awareness. She knew her way around the corridors of power...just as she knew her way around police headquarters.

If no other good came of this summons to Washington, Jack thought grimly, at least it had brought Angela Paretti into his plane of existence, or him into hers. Whatever infinitesimal odds had placed them together on that bridge at that moment in time, the kiss they'd shared owed nothing to chance. He'd wanted it. More than he could remember wanting anything in a long time. She'd wanted it, too. For that brief moment when their breath had mingled and their lips had joined, she'd taken all he gave.

There'd be a next time. Jack didn't know where, or when, or how. But there'd be a next time. First, though, he had to beard her wily boss in his den.

Feeling as frazzled by the day's events as by the man at her side, Angela pushed open a massive mahogany door and ushered her passenger into Senator Claiborne's small kingdom. The cadre of aides and interns who manned the outer office peppered them with excited exclamations.

"Angela! We heard about the shooting!"

"The senator's already expressed his outrage to the mayor."

"Have you called your mother?" an anxious intern asked. "I don't want to be the one to tell her about this!"

"Come on, Angela, give us the details."

"I will, I promise. Later. Let me get the senator's guest settled first."

"Dr. Merritt, your office called to verify your arrival," one of the aides volunteered. "Your assistant couldn't believe it when I told her what had happened. She asked that you give her a call when you can."

"Thanks, I will."

With Jack at her side, Angela crossed the acre of red

carpet to the inner suite of offices. At their entrance, the senator's legislative director shoved his glasses up on his forehead and rose. He strode forward, his thin, intelligent face creased with concern.

"Angela! I couldn't believe it when I heard about the drive-by shooting. Are you all right?"

She plunked her purse on the desk reserved for her use during the long hours she waited for her boss.

"I'm fine, Marc. Still furious at the idea of being used for target practice, and still a little sticky from my whipped-cream facial, but fine."

His sandy brows arched, pushing the wire-rimmed glasses higher on his forehead. "Whipped-cream facial?"

"I'll tell you about it later." She made the necessary introductions. "This is Jack Merritt. Jack, this is Senator Claiborne's legislative director, Marc Green."

If the staffer was surprised that she and her passenger were on a first-name basis, he didn't show it.

"Dr. Merritt…Jack."

Angela watched with some interest as the two men engaged in the curious male greeting ritual that consisted of one part introduction and three parts sizing each other up. While they measured each other, she did a little sizing up of her own.

They both wore the trappings of authority, she thought, contrasting Jack's tailored gray suit with Marc's crisp white shirt and the power suspenders that were the standard uniform for senior staffers on the Hill. Both sported short, ultraconservative haircuts, although Marc's was designed to disguise his thinning sandy hair, while Jack's had been ruthlessly trimmed to a neat black pelt. Both carried themselves with a cool confidence that came from having achieved success in their chosen professions.

Yet for all their similarities, Angela sensed a vital difference in the two men. Jack exuded a quiet, confident authority that came from within. Marc's authority stemmed from his association with the powerful senior senator from South Carolina. It was a subtle difference, one that Angela was surprised she even noticed.

Just when and how had she let herself become so darned aware of Jack Merritt as a man? she thought irritably. And why couldn't she shake the memory of those brief moments in his arms?

"I feel as though we should apologize for that deplorable shooting," Marc said smoothly, pulling her away from the kiss that insisted on lingering in the back of her mind. "You wouldn't have been on that bridge if the Senator hadn't enticed you into coming to Washington."

"Enticed?" Cynical amusement colored Merritt's deep voice. "How about coerced? Your boss has a way with threats."

The aide permitted himself a smile. "True. I'll admit that I tried to talk the senator out of bringing you here. As you yourself pointed out, your data is as yet untested. But now that you're here, I'm anxious to hear what you have to tell us. The system of audits you've instituted at Children's could very well be the model we're looking to include in our medical reform legislation."

"Perhaps the senator should wait until he hears what I have to say before he decides that."

If Angela hadn't worked with Marc Green for almost three years, she might have missed the tiny ripple of annoyance that crossed his face. Obviously he didn't like the subtle reminder that the senator was the one who wielded the power, not him.

Score one for the goat.

"Where is the senator?" she asked, stepping into the breach.

"He got called to the floor for another vote."

"Thank goodness! I figured he'd be chewing his mustache with impatience by now. It took me longer to do that composite than I'd anticipated."

"Composite?" Marc slid his glasses onto his nose. "What composite?"

"I caught a glimpse of the shooter. Barely enough to form an impression, but enough for the police to do a computerized sketch. I'll tell you about it later. In the meantime, why don't you take Jack into the boss's office? I'll join you in a few moments."

She didn't miss Jack's flicker of surprise at the way she included herself in the meeting. Nor did Marc.

"Angela is more than just Senator Claiborne's driver," the aide explained, giving her the private smile that always set her teeth just a little bit on edge. "She often serves as his personal confidante and sounding board."

With an inner sigh, Angela waited for the sudden speculation she knew would spring into Jack's eyes at this vague definition of her duties. She'd seen that look often enough since she began working for the senator. Sometimes she could almost hear the wheels clicking as casual visitors and a disappointing number of insiders mentally translated "driver and personal confidante" into "driver and *very* personal confidante."

Once again, Jack surprised her. Instead of the sly speculation she half expected, his gray eyes reflected only glinting approval.

"It's good to know our elected officials discuss the issues with someone besides other politicians. I'd hate to think their entire view of the world is through these narrow windows."

He was doing it again, Angela thought. Going human on her. If she wasn't careful, she could really start to like this man. The smile she gave him was a few degrees warmer than she'd intended.

"Thanks. I'll be right back. I just have to get the bill for the window replacement to the chief of staff for processing."

"And call your mother," Marc put in. "God forbid she should hear about the shooting from anyone but you."

Sighing, Angela nodded.

The first chore took all of two minutes. She tracked down the senator's busy chief of staff, gave her the details of the harrowing incident and suggested that she process repayment to the city as soon as possible. The administrator grimaced, knowing as well as Angela how little their boss would want to be under any sort of obligation to the mayor.

The second chore took considerably longer. Maria Paretti was by turns shocked, horrified, blazingly angry and adamant in her insistence that her daughter drive up to Baltimore immediately so that her mother could see for herself that she was whole and unharmed. It took some doing, but Angela managed to pacify her with a promise to call again later.

She entered the inner office just as the door leading to a private passageway to the senate floor opened and Henry Claiborne strode in. Not noticing the two men seated at the conference table at the far end of his office, he focused his attention on Angela.

"Well, well, missy," he boomed, crossing the room to take both her hands in his. "What's this 'bout you getting caught in traffic? I never thought I'd live to see the day you stalled out in the middle of the pack."

As always, his presence seemed to shrink the massive proportions of his paneled office. Like Jack Merritt, the senator was a big man, if not as compactly muscled. Age and a well-known partiality for sour-mash bourbon had thickened his once spare frame and added to the heavy jowls that had spawned his famous nickname. He hadn't allowed either time or Mother Nature to dim the luster of his wildly extravagant red mustache, however, or the carroty eyebrows that formed such a startling contrast to his shining bald pate. Now in his early seventies, he was as shrewd as he was ornery and, Angela knew from personal experience, as generous with his personal resources as he was careful with his public trust.

Over the years, his powerful personality had found an outlet in the outrageously exaggerated image of the Suthrun senator that he turned on and off like a faucet. Angela loved his bombast as much as she loved him. Laughing, she gave his gnarled fingers a gentle squeeze.

"I know, I know. The unimaginable has finally occurred. I got stuck in traffic. But if that logjam had happened anywhere else but on the Fourteenth Street Bridge, I would've found a way over, under or around it."

"I can surely give testimony to that." His blue eyes skimmed her face. "I heard the car took a hit, and you hit the bridge. Did either of you sustain any irreparable damage?"

"I'm fine, and the, ah, mayor took it upon himself to have the car windows repaired. Don't worry," Angela assured him hastily. "I've already processed the repayment."

"Good, good! Er, have you called your mother?"

"Yes."

"That's a relief, missy! I surely wouldn't have wanted to be the one to tell her 'bout this little incident." His bluff air fading, he gripped her fingers. "You sure you're all right? No scraped knees or cuts from flyin' glass?"

"No scraped knees or cuts, honest. Jack...that is, Dr. Merritt, shielded me when we ducked for cover. He ended up wearing most of the broken glass."

"He did, did he?"

Giving her hand a final pat, the senator turned his keen gaze on his visitor.

"Well, well, Jack—may I call you Jack?—I invited you to Washington to discuss how your audits might fit into my medical reform program. But your courageous actions today might just give me the ammunition I need to introduce some anticrime legislation. I'm doubly in your debt, sir, doubly."

"I wouldn't call my actions particularly courageous, Senator," Merritt replied dryly. "But you're welcome to make what political hay you can of them."

"Yes, I know."

"You do?"

At the cool lift of his visitor's brow, the senator chuckled and waved Angela to her usual seat at the conference table. Then he settled his bulk in the well-worn leather armchair he'd occupied for four decades.

"I know a good bit about you, sir. Everything my staff could put together on short notice."

"Somehow, that doesn't surprise me."

Leaning back in his chair, Merritt looked as relaxed

as the legislator. For the life of her, Angela couldn't see anything but mild interest in his face.

"Did you learn anything useful, Senator?"

"Indeed I did, sir. Indeed I did. I learned that you left home the day you turned eighteen and served this great nation of ours in the navy. That you went back to school and started as defensive end at Duke. That you turned your back on your grandfather's communications empire and made your own way in this world."

"That's pretty ancient history, Senator."

Smiling genially, the legislator laced his hands over his paunch. "I learned you built up the capital improvement fund at St. Joseph's in Birmingham through shrewd long-term investments. And that you pulled Children's from the fiscal fire when you took over there five years ago. I've also learned that you're stirrin' up a passel of interest throughout the medical community with these audits you've instituted at Children's. I'm looking forward to hearin' more about those audits, son."

The politely couched command hung on the air. Jack took his time responding.

"As I told you over the phone, Senator, the audits were designed as an internal management tool to help us eliminate waste and increase efficiency. The results weren't intended for public dissemination...particularly to outside parties who want to interpret the data in ways that will satisfy personal or political agendas."

Angela blinked. Merritt certainly didn't believe in pulling his punches. Most of the men and women summoned into this office were intimidated by the power and authority of the man who occupied it. Not the chief financial officer and senior vice president of Children's, apparently.

A reluctant admiration for the man sitting across the table stirred in her chest, adding to the pile of emotions he'd been generating in her since she opened her eyes at the airport.

"Well, now, sir," the senator said mildly, "I freely admit to having a political agenda. That's why I occupy this sacred office. But I'm willing to leave the data interpretation to you...for now."

With the last two words, the swords were drawn. Swiftly. Cleanly. Her shoulders tensing, Angela waited for the first clash of steel on steel. She should have remembered that her boss was far too skilled a politician to launch a direct frontal attack.

"Why don't you tell me how these audits of yours work?" he suggested.

Merritt eyed him for a long moment, then reached for his briefcase and pulled out a neat stack of charts.

"Basically, I employ a version of the statistical process control methodology developed by Demming and the total-quality management gurus."

The senator smiled. "You think you might put that in terms this ol' coon dawg might understand?"

The glint in Jack's eyes told Angela he wasn't fooled by his seeming ignorance.

"I've designed a simple computerized program that establishes a statistical norm for certain tasks, then tracks variations from the norm. It's similar to the program the Congressional Budget Office uses to track items such as receipt of honoraria and the use of free mailing privileges by legislators."

"I do believe I'm familiar with that particular program, son."

"I thought you might be."

The senator acknowledged the hit with a dry chuckle.

"So what kind of tasks do you measure with your audits?"

"Anything and everything that might affect our daily operation or the quality of care we provide. As these charts indicate, we're looking at everything from the continuing medical education credits accrued by our consulting physicians to how long it takes maintenance to repair a broken floor tile or change a light bulb."

"Is that so? Just how long does it take to change a light bulb at Children's?"

Evincing a genuine interest, Senator Claiborne talked through the stack of charts with his visitor. Jack Merritt's astonishing grasp of every detail of the hospital's operation added to Angela's sneaking admiration. He was clearly a hands-on manager, and sensitive to the needs of his clients. Unlike a number of his profession she'd had to deal with on her brother's behalf, she admitted grudgingly.

When the last chart lay facedown on the table, the senator stroked his mustache with a liver-spotted hand. From the way his lids drooped under his bushy brows, a casual observer might have supposed he was about to indulge in a midafternoon nap...as he frequently did.

Angela was no casual observer, however. She recognized that slow, caressing stroke. Suddenly her throat went dry. The next few moments would determine whether their sacrificial goat went to the altar willingly or bleating in protest.

"This is all very interestin', son. *Very* interestin'. I'm impressed, especially by the corrective actions you list for those tasks that show variances outside the norm. But surely your audits have discovered some practices that aren't just outside the norm, they're outside the pale."

"We've found a few," Jack admitted, gathering up the charts.

"Like the prescriptions written for Gromorphin?"

His eyes narrowing, Jack met the senator's bland gaze across the expanse of polished table. For long moments, the only sound in the huge office was the loud ticktock of the old-fashioned hunter's clock on the credenza behind the senator's desk.

Angela held her breath. This was the man who had snared her wrist at the airport. Cold. Contained. Distant.

"May I ask what interest you have in a growth hormone, Senator?"

Leaning forward, Marc Green preempted his boss. "Gromorphin is not *a* growth hormone. It's *the* growth hormone. The only one on the market."

"The only synthetic one."

The staffer's mouth thinned at the clipped correction. Marc was rarely corrected, Angela knew. By anyone.

"The only synthetic hormone on the market," he conceded. "It's produced by Miles and distributed exclusively by—"

"Children's is one of the premier centers for the treatment of juvenile growth hormone deficiency," their visitor snapped. "I know who distributes Gromorphin."

He damn well ought to know, Jack thought grimly.

The drug was distributed by HealthMark, the same vast conglomerate that had invited him to conferences in Aruba and Switzerland. The same corporation whose senior sales rep had huddled with a whiskey-voiced blonde in a bar in Tampa. The same company that the Food and Drug Administration's Office of Criminal Investigations had targeted for a secret probe as a result of Jack's audit findings.

He knew who distributed the hormone, all right.

What he didn't know was Senator Claiborne's connection with the pharmaceutical company.

His mind raced with the possibilities that he and the team of special agents working the HealthMark investigation had discussed when the senator's call first came in. The most obvious, of course, was that the potentially explosive audit findings had somehow leaked and Claiborne wanted to use them in his campaign for more government control of drug distribution and sales.

Less obvious was the possibility that the legislator was working a more personal agenda. Like all huge health-related industries, HealthMark had a vital stake in medical reform legislation. Had they contributed under the table to the senator's campaign chest, in the hopes of buying his influence? Had they sponsored *his* attendance at conferences in exotic locations? Were they now calling in their chits, asking Claiborne to exert his influence to discover and perhaps discredit the audit findings?

Since the senator's summons, the investigators had been scrambling to uncover the link, if there was one. So far, they had far more questions than answers.

Jack was still sorting through the possibilities when Angela entered the conversation for the first time. She leaned forward, her dark eyes intent.

"Gromorphin isn't used just to treat growth hormone deficiency in juveniles," she said, gripping her hands together. "The FDA classifies it as a metabolic steroid. It can also be used to reverse acquired GH deficiency in adults, particularly those who have sustained significant damage to their body composition or physical performance."

"Like your brother," Jack said slowly.

"Like my brother."

His reaction was pure instinct, shooting into his gut before his logical mind could break it down and analyze it. He hoped she wasn't part of it. Whatever linked Henry Claiborne to the company now secretly being probed by a team of highly specialized agents, he hoped to hell Angela wasn't part of it.

"Well, now, son," the senator said with unruffled geniality. "We understand one of your audits targeted this particular drug. We would surely like to hear the results of that audit."

"I don't have that information with me," Jack replied slowly. "And even if I did, I'd want to know exactly why you want the information before I shared it."

"Well, sir, you may be familiar with this little bill I've drafted. It's in committee right now, has been for some time. But I'm determined to shake it loose. It contains specific provisions for government oversight into this business of—"

A distinctive pulsing buzz cut the senator off. He glanced over his shoulder at his phone, then heaved himself out of his armchair.

"Excuse me, Angela, gentlemen. I do believe that's the White House callin'. No, no. Keep your seats. I'll let you know if it's a matter that requires privacy."

Turning his back on the other occupants in the room, he contemplated the spectacular view of the Mall outside his windows as he took the call. While Claiborne murmured into the phone, Jack's breath left him in a long, hard rush.

Damn! He felt as though he'd been run over by a careening ambulance. Correction—by a midnight-blue Chrysler driven by a long-haired, heavy-footed female. How in blue blazes had he let himself be blindsided like this? If he'd been thinking clearly, instead of allowing himself to be distracted by little things like a drive-by shooting and a blob of whipped cream on Angela Paretti's left earlobe, he might have made the connection sooner between her brother's injuries and the growth hormone at the center of the investigation that had consumed Jack's days and nights for the past four months.

He knew now that he was bound to Angela by more than just a few moments of violence and intimacy on the Fourteenth Street Bridge. She was part of what had brought him to Washington. The question he wanted answered was how much a part.

He was still trying to sort through the tangled strands that joined him to the woman drumming her fingertips on the conference table when the senator rejoined them, chuckling gleefully.

"Well, well. I do believe we must be gettin' close to an election year. The president wants to hash over a possible compromise on the welfare reform bill with me and the speaker...if we'd be so kind as to join him in his office."

"It's about time he came off his hard line," Marc Green said with a small, tight smile. "I'll get the discussion papers I put together for you that detail the points we're willing to concede."

As the staffer hurried out, the senator turned to Jack. "About this data on this Gromorphin audit, son. I'd surely like you to put it together while I'm gone. We'll talk about it when I get back. Maybe over dinner and—"

"You can't tonight," Angela murmured.

At her boss's blank look, she sighed and lifted a foot. The red hearts on her sneakers glittered merrily.

"It's Valentine's Day, remember? You have another...appointment this evening."

The senator's blue eyes widened. His mustache twitched for a second or two like a squirrel's tail. "That's right! It is!"

Abandoning his air of bluff heartiness, he altered his plans with brisk efficiency. "I'll drive to the White Houser with the speaker. I can go on to my next appointment when I finish there. Angela, you take care of Jack here."

"Me?"

"Take him to his hotel, then to dinner on my account. Talk to him about why we want to see the data he's collected on Gromorphin."

She gave Jack a doubtful glance. "I'm not sure that's a good idea, Senator. Besides, I can't. I promised Gus I'd help him out tonight."

"Now, now, missy. Gus will understand."

"But—"

"You're more familiar with this issue than anyone else on my staff, even Marc. If anyone can convince Dr. Merritt to cooperate, you can. If not—" his blue eyes telegraphed a clear signal that he was playing hard-ball now "—I'll exercise the full power of a congressional subpoena at the hearings."

With a tip of his head to Jack, he hurried out.

His driver watched him leave, a look of mingled exasperation and resignation on her face. Then she folded her arms and turned to survey her assigned project for the evening. A sneakered foot beat impatiently against the carpet.

"Can I? Convince you to cooperate?"

"You can try. You can certainly try."

# Chapter 5

"Who's Gus?"

Jack's question broke the silence that had stretched between him and his reluctant dinner companion since the elevator's descent to the underground parking space.

"My cousin Teresa's husband," Angela replied, twisting the key in the Chrysler's ignition.

"How were you supposed to help him out tonight?"

She waited until she'd negotiated the steep exit ramp and had the car pointed into the stream of traffic to respond.

"Gus is chief dispatcher for Top Hat Limousine Service. He got me a job there a couple of years ago, moonlighting as a driver whenever the senator didn't need me. I don't pull as many gigs as I used to, but I try to help him out on special occasions."

"Special occasions like Valentine's Day?"

"Especially Valentine's Day. This is one of the busiest nights of the year in the limo business." She speared a hand through her hair. "He'll just have to juggle the schedule and double up the other drivers."

With a small frown, Jack recalled Detective Winters's comment about Angela working two jobs to help with her brother's bills.

"I didn't know about your prior commitments when I agreed to the senator's suggestions for tonight. We can skip dinner and meet after you get through work."

She shook her head. "No good. I told Gus I'd take back-to-back gigs. I wouldn't be through until late, well after midnight."

"I'll be awake," Jack drawled.

He sure as hell wasn't going to sleep until he got some answers, and the most pressing question in his mind right now was how much Angela Paretti really knew about HealthMark and Gromorphin.

He wanted to believe that her interest stemmed from her brother's experience and from her own obvious involvement in the senator's reform legislation. He needed to believe it. He still owed her for dragging him out of the line of fire. And, he reminded himself, he had every intention of wangling another kiss. This time with her eyes closed.

"There's another option," she said slowly, almost reluctantly. We could have dinner—and our talk—while my clients are having theirs."

"Won't your customers object to an added passenger?"

"They might, if I took along another passenger." She skimmed him with a quick look. "Your dark suit is close enough to a uniform. We'll scrounge up a hat and make you, um, a driver-in-training."

"A driver-in-training?"

Jack rolled the possibility around in his mind. He

didn't like the idea of sharing Angela's time or attention with her customers. Not with what was at stake.

All right, he admitted silently, he didn't like the idea of sharing her time or attention at all. He wanted her focused on him. Totally. Exclusively.

Angela wasn't surprised when Jack hesitated. She'd suspected before she made the offer that he wouldn't take her up on it, even though it wasn't as off-the-wall as it probably sounded to him.

Most of the limo drivers she worked with bent the rules on occasion to accommodate personal situations. Just last week, one desperate father had tucked his sleeping child into a car seat until his wife finished work. A number of drivers arranged for their girlfriends to meet them and help pass the idle hours of waiting while clients lingered over dinner or sat in a darkened theater.

Usually, Angela took advantage of the downtime to hit the books. She was only eight credit hours away from finally finishing her interrupted master's program. Knowing that the senator would be occupied for the evening, she'd accepted back-to-back gigs tonight with the intent of pulling in some needed cash and using the idle time to cram for an upcoming exam.

She might still get in her study time. A quick glance at her passenger told her that he had some doubts about his proposed change in status.

"What kind of hat would I have to wear?" he asked cautiously.

"A top hat. It's not just the name of the service," she said primly, "it's part of our professional image."

She fully expected him to back out now. She wouldn't blame him. Every one of the drivers at Top Hat hated the ridiculous headgear. Angela couldn't see a vice president and chief financial officer agreeing to wear one while he tooled around D.C. as a driver-in-training.

She bit back a sigh. She hated to disappoint Gus. He needed her help tonight.

On the other hand, she acknowledged silently, an evening spent in Jack Merritt's exclusive company wouldn't exactly constitute a fate worse than death. As reluctant as she was to admit it, there was more between them at this point than politics.

Maybe they *had* invested something in each other during those few moments on the Fourteenth Street Bridge. Maybe it *was* time to explore the heightened, prickly awareness that gripped her every time she and Jack Merritt occupied the same airspace.

She felt it now. A curious sort of crowding of her senses, as though she couldn't draw a breath without taking in his scent, or shift in her seat without touching him. She had a crazy, disturbing urge to do just that…breathe him. Touch him. Take him up on his offer to try another kiss, this time with her eyes closed.

His deep voice broke into her swirling thoughts. "If they have a hat that will fit me, I'll try to live up to your professional image."

Angela curled her fingers around the wheel. A small pleasure darted down her spine at his willingness to accommodate himself to her schedule.

"Oh, I'm pretty sure we can find one to fit."

She knew for a fact that they had a whole locker full of the silly things at central dispatch.

"What time's your first gig?"

She darted a quick look at the digital clock above the instrument panel. "At 6:30. We just have time to swing by your hotel and get you checked in. We'll have to make tracks from there, though.''

"My reservation's confirmed with a credit card. We don't need to go by the hotel.''

"Hold on, then.''

Flicking a look in the rear and side mirrors, Angela veered across the lanes of traffic. A black-shod foot beside hers thumped the floor mat reflexively. This time, she didn't bother to hide her smile.

"Here's your first lesson, trainee. A good driver always knows what's behind, beside and ahead. He can thread his car through an opening the size of a lug nut, if necessary, and not scrape the paint.''

"Let's hope it doesn't become necessary tonight,'' Jack drawled.

The ready laughter that was as much a part of Angela's nature as her occasionally volatile temper bubbled in her throat. She took her gaze from the road for a moment and caught an answering glimmer in his eyes. As it had before, his amusement pulled at something inside her.

Suddenly, her awareness of the man beside her changed gears, shifting out of prickly and slipping into shivery with the smooth precision of a short-block engine. Angela felt its powerful thrust to the tips of her sneakered toes. Taking a firm grip on her emotions and the wheel, she weaved through the rush-hour-clogged streets.

Twenty minutes later, she turned off Wisconsin Avenue into Top Hat's lot. Protected on the street side by a chain-link fence, the lot was shielded on the other three sides by tall buildings. The Chrysler slid to a halt with its front bumper a scant inch from a brick wall.

"I'll be right back. I just have to pick up the trip

tickets and the keys. And our hats," she added with a grin.

"You sure having me ride shotgun won't get you in trouble?"

"Not with Gus," she said simply. "He's family."

A cold wind swirled her skirt as she swung her legs out of the car. The unseasonable February warmth had fallen victim to the early-evening shadows now creeping across the yard. Turning up the collar of her black wool tunic against the chill, Angela hurried toward the dilapidated metal shack that Top Hat's owner pretentiously called the dispatch center.

She was back at the Chrysler a few moments later, a clipboard and two flattened black silk disks clutched to her chest. Merritt joined her outside, his dark hair ruffling in the nippy breeze.

"Here, try this one for size."

A smart smack on her forearm popped one of the flattened disks into its full glory. She handed it to Jack, who tilted it to a jaunty angle above his right eyebrow.

"What do you think?"

"I think you look very—" she struggled for the right words "—very debonair."

"That bad, huh?"

No, Angela thought breathlessly. That good. That incredibly good.

Somehow, he managed to carry off the ridiculous headgear with a panache that Cary Grant might have envied. It gave him a decidedly aristocratic air, and drew Angela's attention to the strong, lean lines of his face. His very attractive face.

Good grief! What was the matter with her? She'd met this man for the first time this morning. Then, her sole concern had been delivering him into the senator's clutches. Now, she was in serious danger of forgetting her primary mission tonight. Yanking herself back to reality, she plopped on her own hat and checked the keys clamped to the clipboard.

"We've got 286. It's a slug, but it's clean."

A quick search of the lot located the silver Lincoln Town Car with the sixty-inch presidential stretch. Pulling a pen out of her purse, Angela anchored the fluttering trip tickets with her thumb.

"Okay, our first gig is a deluxe package with dinner and a moonlight tour. I'll read the options the customers have requested, you check to see if they're in place."

"You're taking my role as your trainee seriously, aren't you?"

"You might as well be useful, as well as decorative. One red rose in a silver vase." She pointed to the limo with her pen. "Check it out."

Jack removed his hat and stuck his head in the rear door. "One red rose in a silver vase. Check."

"Champagne—Dom Pérignon '83. On ice."

"Check. Not a particularly good year, by the way."

She ignored the editorial comment. "Four champagne flutes."

"Why four?"

"In case of breakage. Are they there?"

"Check."

"One cassette tape... Wait, it's here on the clipboard. Oh, gag! Rachmaninoff. That's about as fresh and original as used crankcase fluid."

"What would you consider appropriate to the occasion?" Jack asked curiously, slamming the rear door shut.

She cocked her head, thinking. "Caruso, in his later

years. Lanza in some of his earlier recordings. Pavarotti, anytime.''

"I see. Italian tenors seem to have the edge in the romance department.''

"In my family, they do,'' she replied breezily, scanning the second trip ticket. Her face fell when she saw the name and pickup address on the ticket. "Oh, no! I can't believe Gus stuck me with the Browser again!''

"Who or what is the Browser?''

"He's a regular. Unfortunately.''

"I don't think I like the sound of this.''

"Don't worry. I can handle him...as long as I'm wearing gloves when I do it.''

While her assistant pondered that one, Angela slipped into the driver's seat and started the engine. The Lincoln turned over with a low, cultured rumble. Leaving the car in park, she performed a quick walkaround to check the tires, lights and directional signals. Then she buckled herself in and gripped the wheel.

"Ready for your first gig as a semiprofessional chauffeur, Dr. Merritt?''

"As ready as I'll ever be.''

They were driving out of the lot when Angela caught a muted chuckle coming from the far side of the front seat.

"What?'' she asked, effortlessly adjusting the turn radius to the Lincoln's extended length.

"I was just remembering the complimentary package the travel agency put together for me for this trip to Washington. As I recall, the package included a limo, chilled champagne, and a moonlight tour of D.C. in lights.''

"No kidding? Hey, Gus might have a trip ticket that

says you should be sitting in the back seat instead of the front.''

"I don't think so. I instructed my assistant to make sure Gulliver's Travels canceled the package.''

"Why?''

"I didn't think it appropriate for the person responsible for Children's fiscal resources to tool around Washington in a limo.''

She smiled across the small space between them. "And here you are.''

He nodded, his gaze settling on her face in a way that raised goose bumps on Angela's arms. "Here I am.''

By the time he'd seated her at a small table in a crowded, noisy basement cantina a few blocks from the elegant Georgetown restaurant where their clients were dining, Jack had begun to seriously regret his decision to accompany Angela on her gigs.

He was hungry, rib-knocking hungry, and listening to Rachmaninoff played repeatedly all the way in from Bethesda had given him an acute dislike of a composer he'd always enjoyed before. He'd also discovered that being squeezed into Angela's busy schedule left him wanting more. More of her time. More of her attention. More of the generous smiles she bestowed on clients, doormen and waiters alike...including the one who hovered over them now.

"You want the usual, Angelina?''

"Yes, please, Dominic. But hold the pine nuts.''

"And you, sir?''

"I'll have the same.''

"Primo! Two *fettuccine con salsa di noci*.'' The swarthy waiter hurried off, beaming.

"Do you have any idea what you just ordered?" Angela asked curiously.

"No. Will I like it?"

"You'll love it. It's the house specialty. Homemade noodles with pureed walnuts, ricotta and fresh Parmesan in a cream sauce. Dominic's father guards the recipe like the family honor."

"Are Dominic and his father your cousins?"

"Mmm…more like cousins-in-law, three or four times removed," she replied, rummaging around in her purse. She fished out a black beeper, which she laid on the checkered tablecloth, presumably so that she could hear it over the clatter of cutlery and the animated conversations that buzzed through the cramped restaurant.

"Why do I get the feeling you're related to half the population of Washington?"

Her mouth curved. "It certainly feels like it sometimes. My great-grandparents settled in South Philly when they first immigrated, but the Parettis spread like the plague up and down the East Coast. When I moved down here from Baltimore, which is where my folks live, my mother alerted all the aunts and uncles and cousins in the area to keep an eye on me. They still report back to her on a regular basis."

"Sounds like she takes her maternal duties very seriously."

"She does. Believe me, she does! If I don't check in with her at least once a day, she activates a security alert system the Pentagon would envy."

The brown eyes across from Jack spilled over with an affectionate exasperation that didn't diminish the love behind it.

"She refuses to accept the fact that her twenty-nine-year-old daughter has left the nest. She swears she won't be able to sleep peacefully until I bring home a husband who meets with her approval, preferably one of Italian-American extraction.''

"Have you brought any who didn't meet with her approval?''

"No." She plucked a breadstick out of a group nestled in a tall glass and crunched off a tip. "I came close once, though. The summer I turned eighteen. I fell madly in love with a mechanic who'd just joined Tony's crew.''

A sudden image of an eighteen-year-old Angela, head over heels in love, her eyes luminous with pleasure, her body warm and pliant, sent a spiral of heat curling through Jack's belly. Accompanying the heat came a fierce, unreasoning jealousy of the nameless, faceless mechanic.

"Unfortunately, my brother discovered before I did that the jerk had a wife and a couple of kids in Cleveland. When Tony got through with him, he was *not* a pretty sight.''

"Good for Tony.''

She took another crunch, then propped her chin in her hands. "What about you, Jack? How many women did you bring home for your family's approval?''

"My parents died when I was a kid. I lived with my grandfather until I went into the navy, and we rarely saw eye-to-eye on anything, much less my taste in women. But I suppose that was covered in some detail in the senator's report,'' he added deliberately.

She didn't evade the issue. "Yes, it was.''

The reminder of the unresolved business that lay between them killed their companionable ease. Jack regretted its loss, but he knew he had only these few hours to learn what he could of Angela's role in the spiraling web that had ensnared him.

"What else was in the report?" he asked her.

"The basics."

"Tell me."

"Name, Jonathan Calder Merritt. Age, thirty-six. Height, six-one. Weight, 183 at the time of your last driver's-license renewal. Divorced, no children. Three advanced degrees in accounting and business management. Several years' apprenticeship at Price Waterhouse, specializing in health care consortiums and stock bundles. Comptroller at St. Joseph's in Mobile..."

"Birmingham."

The breadstick swooped through the air like a salty baton. "Birmingham. Then Children's, and these audits, and Gromorphin."

"Right. Gromorphin." Jack willed himself to keep his voice even. "How much do you know about the drug, Angela?"

"I know—"

Dominic interrupted, presenting two earthenware bowls with a flourish. "Your salad."

The question hung between them until the waiter had grated fresh Parmesan on the salads and plunked a basket of fresh bread on the table. Angela smiled her thanks, then returned to the issue at hand.

"I know a treatment regimen of one shot a day costs sixty to seventy thousand dollars a year."

"At a minimum."

"I know that HealthMark, which distributes Gromorphin, took in over a billion dollars in revenues last year just from their drug distribution unit."

"So I understand."

She leaned forward, the half-eaten breadstick still

clutched in one fist. "I don't know, but I suspect that certain endocrinologists receive hundreds of thousands of dollars in kickbacks for prescribing the expensive drug. Endocrinologists like the one Tony was referred to."

Jack went still. She didn't know.

She suspected, but she didn't know.

The high wire stretched before him, tight, quivering. He kept silent, letting her step out onto the wire as far as she would.

"The doctor my brother was referred to prescribed a treatment regimen that would've lasted six months longer than Tony really needed, Jack. Six months."

The breadstick crumbled in her hands.

"Tony refused the treatment. We didn't find out until later that he based his decision on the cost of the drug, not his need. My father... Well, he came up with the money, but by then Tony had found another endocrinologist. This doctor didn't actually admit it, but he implied that the first physician had a reputation for extending the treatment schedules beyond what might be required."

"If that's true," Jack said slowly, watching her eyes, "it's a matter for criminal prosecution, not congressional debate."

"Then why isn't it being prosecuted?" she shot back.

"How do you know it isn't?"

"Because I checked. I asked questions. I learned everything I could about Gromorphin." She drew in a deep breath. "In the process, I discovered that your audits of prescriptions written for this particular drug were causing a quiet uproar in certain neuroendrocrinology clinics. That some people were getting very nervous about the results. We want you to tell us what you found, Jack."

"Why?"

"Why not? Why wait until the senator pulls it out of you, bit by bit, in front of the subcommittee?"

"That's not good enough. Tell me why the subcommittee needs the data from this particular audit of this particular drug."

"All right. I'll tell you why. Because growth hormones are among the most expensive drugs on the market. Which makes them prime targets for overprescription. Which leads to abuse and, we think, corruption. Which makes the case for tighter government controls on these and other high-cost pharmaceuticals."

Jack saw the passionate conviction in her eyes. Heard the absolute sincerity ringing in her voice. Every instinct he possessed told him she was sincere. Whatever Senator Claiborne's motivation was for wanting the audit results, his driver was squarely on the side of the consumer.

Muscle by taut muscle, Jack relaxed. He could more than hold his own in any debate on medical reform.

"Increased government regulation won't necessarily improve the health care system."

"It can't make it much worse," she retorted.

"I have a good idea what you went through after your brother's accident," he began slowly.

"This isn't about me. Or Tony. Or my family. We managed. It was tough, but we managed."

For once, her hands were still as her curled fists rested on either side of her plate.

"This is about a flawed system. From what we understand, you've found evidence that substantiates some of the most serious flaws. You. Not an outsider. Not a patient. Not an insurance adjudicator or a Medicare investigator. You found it, and your findings have credibility because they come from within.''

''But that's the crux of the matter,'' Jack returned. ''Isn't it? I'm part of the system, flawed though it may be, and I'm not convinced that it can be fixed through more government regulation and control. So convince me, Angela.''

''Have you read the senator's proposed legislation?''

''I've read a detailed analysis of it.''

''Prepared by someone in the medical community, right?''

He conceded the point with a nod.

''Well, I just might be able to present a less biased anaylsis.''

Jack sat back as she rooted around in the formless suitcase she called a purse, then flopped a dog-eared bound copy of Senate Bill 693 on the table. As she launched into a detailed summary of its key features, a fleeting sense of unreality gripped him. Here he was, sitting across from the most intriguing woman he'd met in years, debating the pros and cons of government oversight of the health care industry over homemade noodles and Caesar salad.

There was something wrong with this picture, he thought wryly. Seriously wrong.

''The senator wants the specific facts and figures, Jack. He wants to show instances of flagrant abuse to support his—''

Her beeper sounded, cutting her off in midargument. She glanced at the digital readout and scrambled for her purse.

''It's the headwaiter across the street. Grab your hat. Time to get back to work.''

He rose, reaching for both his hat and his wallet.

"No, no." She waved his money away. "This is on the senator."

"I don't think so." He dropped two twenties on the table. "I'm the one who worries about appearances, remember?"

"You can't worry about them too much," she tossed back with a quicksilver grin. "How many people do you see walking around town in a top hat?"

By necessity, they suspended their discussion of medical reform during the deluxe moonlight tour of Washington.

Angela proved an excellent tour guide. She was by turns cheerful and full of information when the couple in the back seat asked for it and discreetly quiet when they nestled in each other's arms to peer out at the floodlit sights.

Smiling, she offered Jack a percentage of their clients' generous tip. When he declined, she picked up the debate where they'd left off an hour ago.

Both her smile and her animated arguments faded when they picked up the Browser. Concave-chested and reeking of a noxious aftershave that barely disguised an equally noxious body odor, the man had more money than he did hair and, as Angela put it tersely, less personality than a crescent wrench.

The client's face fell to the knees of his baggy pants when he spotted Jack. Pursing his mouth in disapproval, he climbed into the back of the limo and instructed Angela to take it slow around DuPont Circle. The tinted panel separating the passenger compartment from the front seat whirred up, thankfully shutting out most of his overpowering scent. Angela took care of the rest

with a few strategic squirts from a can of air freshener
she fished out of the dash compartment.

"What's he doing back there?" Jack asked as the
limo crept around the small, handsome park where three
of Washington's main thoroughfares and half a dozen
lesser streets converged.

"Browsing," she replied succinctly.

Forehead furrowed, Jack surveyed the wedge-shaped
buildings constructed on the slices of property between
the busy streets leading into the circle. One or two of
the buildings retained traces of their former days of
glory, when DuPont Circle had been lined with resi-
dential mansions, but most had given way to restaurants, off-beat shops and specialty bookstores. Even at
this late hour, the shops and restaurants were filled with
the after-theater set.

Not just the after-theater set, he suddenly realized.
His gaze narrowed on a striking miniskirted brunette
bending over to chat with the driver of the Mercedes
that had pulled up to the curb just ahead. The petite,
ebony-skinned woman standing next to her zinged a
dazzling smile over the hood of the Mercedes at the
limo.

A barked order came over the intercom. "Slower! Go
slower!"

Jack shot Angela an incredulous look. "I hope to hell
Top Hat's services don't include pimping for that character in the back!"

"Of course not! He just likes to look. A lot." Sighing, she began another slow circuit. "Four hours' worth,
at a hundred and fifty dollars an hour."

They drove back to Top Hat's lot long hours later,
with the rear windows wide open to the air and the front

heater going full blast. Throughout the short trip, Jack struggled with a primitive, protective streak that was growing wider with each passing hour in Angela's company. The idea of her having to put up with the likes of the Browser bothered him. Big-time. Almost as much as the idea of her roaming D.C.'s streets in the middle of the night.

He knew damn well his urge to shield her from the Browsers of the world was irrational. He'd met her less than twelve hours ago, for pity's sake. And Angela Paretti wasn't the kind of woman who wanted to be protected from anything. Still, when they finally climbed out of the limo, he slammed the door with more force then necessary.

"Does your mother know what kind of customers you haul around?"

"Good Lord, no! That's between Gus and me. And Tony. He taught me a few interesting moves to take care of characters like Browser."

"Is that right?" Jack knew his voice had an edge to it, but he couldn't seem to shake it.

"That's right," she replied, digging into her purse for the keys to the Chrysler. "I came pretty close to giving you a demonstration on the bridge this afternoon."

"Why didn't you?"

"I don't know." She fumbled with the keys, then aimed the starter at the distant sedan. "You go get warm in the car. I'll turn in the keys and take you back to—"

His hand closed over hers, stilling it. "Why didn't you, Angela?"

She frowned up at him. "I told you, I don't know."

"Think about it."

"You took me by surprise, okay? My heart was still pumping pure adrenaline."

"What's it doing now?"

Her eyes flared, then narrowed dangerously. Before she could let loose with the scathing retort he saw forming on her lips, he lifted her hand and laid it against his sternum.

"Mine's been jumping its tracks all day. And night. The Browser just about toppled it right off the rails. I wanted to do something very unaccountant-like tonight, about the third or fourth time we took him around the circle."

"Why, Dr. Merritt, I do believe that's a real emotion I feel beating in your breast."

"Very real."

Angela caught her breath at the husky rasp in his voice. The shivery awareness that had percolated just below the surface of her skin all evening heated.

"Careful, Merritt. You just might make me believe you're human after all."

"I might at that. Want to try again, Angela? Eyes closed this time?"

The heat dancing under her skin burst into flames. Fire raced along her nerve endings, fanned by the drumming of Jack's pulse beneath her fingertips. Valiantly Angela tried to douse the brushfire before it got out of control.

"I don't think this is a good idea."

"I do. In fact, I can't think of a better one, given the occasion."

"What occasion?"

His eyes danced. "Valentine's Day."

"I hate to be the one to break it to you, but Valentine's Day ended sometime during our fourth or fifth circuit of DuPont Circle.''

''Then we'd better make up for lost time.''

Wrapping his free arm around her waist, he brought her up against him. The hand still covering hers was trapped between their bodies. Jack felt the flutter of her fingers as they flattened against his chest, and the sharp end of a key digging into his breastbone.

This time, he didn't take it slow and easy. This time, he didn't give her the option of drawing away at the last moment. And this time, he noted with soaring, searing elation, she closed her eyes.

When her mouth molded to his, the world exploded around them.

Literally.

For one crazy instant, they stared at each other, not understanding what had happened. Then shock waves reverberated across the lot, and flames lit the night sky.

Distance and several rows of parked limos had saved them from the effects of the blast, but still, they hit the ground. Instinctively. Automatically. For the second time in less than twenty-four hours.

# Chapter 6

Hands on hips, Ed Winters surveyed the Chrysler's twisted, smoldering remains. His lips pursed in a long, soundless whistle.

"I don't think the mayor can fix it this time, Angie."

"I don't think anyone can," she replied morosely. "There's not enough left to salvage for parts."

Hunching her shoulders, she tried to hold in the warmth of Jack's body. Someone had draped a worn football jacket over her shoulders—one of the drivers who'd come running at the sound of the explosion, she thought. But Jack's arm had remained wrapped around her from the moment they picked themselves up off the ground. She didn't even try to pretend that it wasn't welcome.

Winters's gaze ranged to the man beside her. In the glare of the flashing lights from the police cruisers, the detective's face could have been chipped from black granite.

"This hasn't been your lucky day, has it, Merritt?"

"Let's just say it's been interesting."

"You two want to fill me in on a few details? Like what you're doing in the Top Hat parking lot at 3:00 a.m.? And where you've been tonight? And what the hell happened here?"

Angela swept her palm across her forehead in a useless attempt to keep her tangle of windswept hair out of her eyes. This afternoon, she'd felt a scorching fury at the random violence that had touched her. Now, she felt only stunned confusion.

"It's too cold to answer questions out here," Jack interjected. "I suggest we move this discussion to the dispatch center."

"Yeah, you're right." Winters signaled to his partner, a stoop-shouldered veteran in a tan overcoat. "We can go over the witness statements inside, Lowrey. Tell the uniforms to let us know when the bomb squad gets here."

As she turned to leave, Angela took a last look over her shoulder at the charred, blackened wreckage. For an eerie instant, the February chill took on a muggy, humid heat. The scents of benzene fumes, axle grease and male sweat clogged her senses. Once again, she stood transfixed beside the other members of Tony's crew as emergency vehicles converged on a billowing column of black smoke. The acrid taste of terror rose in her throat.

Then Jack's voice penetrated the smoke. Calm. Steady. An anchor in a spiraling, swirling vortex.

"Let's go inside, Angela."

She gave herself a little shake and turned her back on what remained of the Chrysler.

Her cousin's husband met them at the door to the dispatch center. Worry carved deep grooves into a face rounded by years of her cousin Teresa's pasta. Gus had raced to her side mere seconds after the explosion, and returned to dispatch only when a police officer asked to review the logs for the night.

Easing out of Jack's hold, Angela summoned a lopsided grin. "Too bad it wasn't 286 that went up, Gus. That slug should have been put out to pasture years ago. Can we use your office for a while?"

"Sure, sure. There's coffee in there. Help yourself. And when you get through, for God's sake, call your mother! If she hears about this on the morning news, she's gonna kill somebody. Most likely me!"

The tiny glassed-in cubicle barely held the four of them. Angela perched on the phone console and declined Jack's offer of coffee with the warning that Gus's brew could strip paint faster than any solvent known to man. Ed Winters closed the door and wedged sideways to take the chair the others declined.

"Okay, Angie. Start with the explosion. Tell me in your own words what happened."

"There's not much to tell. I used the remote ignition device to start the engine, and the car blew up."

"How does this device work?"

She dragged the Chrysler's keys out of the pocket of the football jacket and passed them over. "It sends a radio signal, just like a garage-door opener or TV remote. You click once to unlock the doors, a second time to start the engine."

Winters stretched out his arm, aiming at the far wall. "So you just pointed at the car and pressed?"

"More or less."

"More or less what?"

"I, uh, didn't exactly point it and I'm not sure who pressed."

He lowered his arm. "I'm missing something here."

"The device was in my hand, which was caught between Jack and me, and we both...sort of pressed."

"Is that so?"

The detective's gaze drifted to the man sipping coffee from a chipped green mug. Tilting his chair back on two legs, he came as close as a police officer allowed himself to a smirk.

"You both just sort of...pressed?"

"Look, Eddie," Angela said impatiently, "it wasn't what you think. Okay, maybe it was. But can we focus a little more on the fact that the senator's car just went up in flames here?"

She wasn't ready to admit to Eddie or anyone else how close she'd come to going up in flames, too. That explosive kiss couldn't have lasted more than a few seconds, yet its heat had blazed a fiery path to her every extremity.

Angela remembered her toes curling in her sneakers and her fingertips sinking into the springy hair at the back of Jack's neck. She remembered closing her eyes and opening her mouth to his. Seconds, or maybe hours, later, the Chrysler had lifted off the ground.

She had a feeling that this Valentine's Day would stay etched in her memory for a long, long time.

"All right," Winters said, bringing the front legs of his chair to the floor with a thump. "We know how the bomb went off...sort of. We know where and when. We won't know what kind of explosive we're talking about until the bomb squad does their thing. So that leaves the why and the who."

"Who planted the bomb, you mean?" Angela threw him an exasperated look. "If we knew that, we wouldn't be sitting here, would we?"

"Not only who planted it," Winters said gently. "Who it was intended to take out."

She sucked in a quick breath. Involuntarily her gaze flew to Jack. His jaw flexed, but he didn't say anything. His turn would come, she knew. Dragging in a deep breath, she tried to bring some order to the thoughts that had tumbled chaotically through her mind since the Chrysler exploded.

"I was the target, Or Jack. Or the senator. The bomb could have contained a delayed timing device that the remote shorted."

Ed nodded. "That's a possibility. Where is the senator tonight?"

"He had an engagement. He told me to use the car, since he wouldn't need it, and take Jack to dinner."

"Then you dropped by Top Hat to visit Gus?"

"No, I took a couple of gigs to help out. You know how it is on Valentine's, Eddie. Jack went out with me as, uh, driver-in-training, and we left the Chrysler at the lot."

"I see." Winters's tone said clearly that he didn't, but he let it pass. "Any ideas why, Angie? Why you? Why Jack, or the senator?"

"None that make any sense."

"Try me."

She flung out a hand, almost dislodging the football jacket. "This is crazy, I know, but the only thing I could think of is that this incident is related to the drive-by shooting. Maybe the shooter heard that I was the one who identified him and did the composite. Maybe he got my name, and somehow tracked me down."

"And maybe the shooting wasn't a drive-by," Winters's partner put in.

Shocked, Angela whirled to face him. "What?"

"You could have been the target of that hit all along. Or Dr. Merritt here. Or maybe it was just a warning."

"A warning? What kind of a warning?"

The older man shrugged. "Everyone knows about your family's troubles, Ms. Paretti. Maybe someone was trying to send your brother a message."

"My brother!"

Winters threw the sloop-shouldered cop a frown. "What the hell are you talking about, Lowrey?"

"It's possible, is all I'm saying. How much did Tony Paretti cost his backers when he cracked up that fancy race car? Who backed him, anyway? Racing's gotten big, too big for organized crime to keep their fingers out of. Maybe there was some 'family' money involved, money that hasn't been repaid, and Ms. Paretti here—"

"You bastard!"

Angela launched herself off the console, fury in every fiber of her being. The older detective almost tripped over his feet as he scrambled backward.

"It's possible, is all I'm saying."

She put herself right in his face. "And you're a flat-footed idiot, is all *I'm* saying."

"Jesus, Lowrey." Shaking his head, Winters tugged her away from his partner. "Calm down, Angie. We're just talking things through here, thinking out loud."

"I don't want that kind of talking or thinking about my family!"

She glared at the older man, who matched her glower for glower but wisely refrained from further comment.

"He's right."

Jack's comment fell like a stone in the heated silence.

"There's a possibility that a professional might be behind both incidents."

All three antagonists spun around to stare at him.

Surprise blanked Lowrey's face. Suspicion sharpened Winters's. And unrelenting hostility etched Angela's into a mask of anger.

"If you think my brother—anyone in my family!— owes anything to the Mafia, you're crazy. Worse than crazy. You're—"

Jack caught her hands at the top of a wild arc. Gripping them tightly in his own, he abruptly altered the rules he'd been playing by for the past four months.

"I'm not talking about the mob."

"Then what? Who?"

"Another organization. Not as powerful, maybe, but desperate. I didn't make the connection this afternoon. All the evidence pointed to a drive-by shooting. The green shirt. The talk of gang initiations. The random path of the bullets."

Jack's jaw clenched. He wasn't going to forgive himself for this afternoon. Or for tonight. Not for a long, long time. He should have known that shooting was anything but random. Should have rejected the flimsy evidence that supported the gang initiation theory. Instead, he'd let himself fall into a deadly trap.

He'd been too caught up in a damned paper investigation! They all had, he and the team of highly skilled special agents he'd been working with. They'd been using financial analyses and computer printouts and telephone records to unravel a tangled web of kickbacks and phony research grants and "consulting fees." Because the suspects tangled in this ever-expanding web were highly placed drug company executives and respected physicians and, possibly, legislators, they'd let the paper chase blind them to the desperate stakes involved.

Jack had questioned HealthMark's willingness to pay

his way to "conferences" at exotic locations. He had suspected the company was behind the offer to play games that the blonde in Tampa whispered in his ear. But he hadn't believed the company might resort to more violent means to take him down. He wouldn't make that mistake again.

And he wouldn't forgive himself for pulling Angela into the morass that sucked at him. Ever.

His gut instincts had told him she wasn't part of the ever-widening circle of corruption he'd stumbled into. When the Chrysler's hood blew off and the car lifted into the air tonight, instinct had convulsed into absolute certainty. Whoever wanted to silence him had decided Angela was expendable, too.

Dragging his gaze from her stunned face, he pinned Winters with a hard look. "How long will it take the bomb squad to do their thing?"

"Two, maybe three hours on-site, then a day or more at the lab. You got something you want to tell me about this, Merritt?"

"I can't tell you anything, but I know someone who can. Call Special Agent Manny Rameriz at the FDA's Office of Criminal Investigations in Miami. Tell him what happened and fill him in on both incidents."

Winters rocked back on his heels. "The FDA, huh? You working for the feds?"

"I'm working with them." He transferred his grip from Angela's hands to her elbow and reached for the door. "Tell Manny I'll get back to him as soon as I can."

"Where do you think you're going?" Lowrey demanded.

"To someplace safe, and you're going to provide a police escort to make sure we get there," Jack growled.

"Until we know for sure who planted that bomb and why, we're laying low."

Winters nodded. "Until we know for sure, that's what I would recommend."

Angela listened with a growing sense of disbelief. Since she'd met Jack Merritt, her world seemed to be spinning out of control.

"Wait a minute."

Her protest went unheeded as Jack edged her out of the tiny office, Winters hard on his heels.

"We maintain a safe house," the detective said. "We can put you up there."

Angela dug in her heels. "Hey! Throttle back here, guys."

She waited until she had their attention, then grabbed at the control that had slipped away from her. "Tell me about this safe house, Eddie."

"We keep it for snitches. Sometimes the streets get too hot and they need a place to hide for a while. We'll lock you up nice and tight, bring your meals. You won't have to step outside until we're sure it's safe."

"I don't like it."

Lowrey gave her a tight, disgruntled look. "What's not to like?"

"I don't like being locked up," she shot back. "I don't like being without wheels, and I don't like staying someplace where snitches have been known to camp out. How long do you think it would take for our location to leak?"

"We haven't lost one of our stoolies in years," Lowrey tossed back, offended.

"Right!"

"This is your turf," Jack interjected. "You pick the spot you'll feel safest."

Angela thought for less than two seconds. Then she strode across the room and stopped in front of the wide-eyed dispatcher.

"We need a car, Gus. Not a limo. Something dark and fast."

"A car? Sure, sure, take my Chevy. It's parked right outside the door." He dug in his pocket and dropped the keys into her palm. "But...but what's going on here, Angela?"

"I don't know."

She started for the door.

Gus hurried alongside her. "But...what's the story on the limo?"

"I don't know."

"But...what are we gonna tell your mother?"

She groaned. "I don't know!"

"Call her," Gus begged as she walked out the door. "You call her, Angela! Please! Before she calls here!"

She stepped out into a cold, clear night marred by the stench of burning rubber and the crackle of radios from the police and fire department vehicles on the scene.

"Is this Gus's car?" Jack asked.

She tore her eyes from the remains of the Chrysler, still smoldering in the distance. With a mental shake, she reached for the door handle of the dark green Chevy.

"Yes."

Ed Winters turned up his coat collar against the cold. "Hang loose, Angie. I'll get a couple of the cruisers to ride shotgun for you. I want to make sure you're not followed."

For the first time since the Chrysler went up in flames, Angela smiled. "No one's going to follow me,

Eddie. Not for long, anyway. Gus has a mobile phone in his car. If I need help, I'll call for the cavalry.''

No one followed them.

Gus's Chevy handled like a dream, which wasn't surprising, since Tony had rebuilt the engine just last year. Cutting corners like a knife, it sped through the streets with a silent tread.

Angela kept one eye on the rearview mirror, both hands on the wheel, and her foot just heavy enough on the gas not to call attention to their swift passage. They'd traveled through the dark, sleeping city and were heading east on Highway 50 before Jack asked the obvious question.

"Where are we going?"

"My uncle has a cabin on Maryland's western shore. It's not much more than a crab shanty, but it's well off the beaten track, and it's safe."

"Does it have a telephone? I don't want to rely on this mobile phone if someone's scanning the airwaves for us."

She nodded. "There's a phone."

"And a bed?"

Her pointed silence lasted for two blocks.

"It's after three," Jack said with exaggerated patience. "I've been up since five this morning. Yesterday morning. You've probably been up as long, if not longer. We need someplace safe to talk through what's happened today. We need to make some calls. Then we both need sleep. Does this crab shanty have a bed?"

"It has a bed. More or less."

Forty minutes later, Jack stepped out of the Chevy and swept the cottage perched precariously above the

Chesapeake with a narrow, searching gaze. Only the rush of the wind through the trees and the slap of the bay against the bank disturbed the dark silence.

Angela groped under a loose shutter for the key, then pushed inside and fumbled for the light switch. A single overhead bulb illuminated a one-room cabin, which was filled with a comfortable clutter of old magazines, red buoys and wooden decoys in various stages of carving and scattered magazines. Half the main room served as a kitchen, the other half as the bedroom-sitting area. An open door in the far wall showed a glimpse of a tiny bathroom.

With a brisk competence, Angela soon had the cabin's gasoline heater going. Within minutes, the interior lost its musty dampness and the room grew warm enough for her to shed her borrowed football jacket and wool tunic.

Jack's breath caught right below his belt buckle at his first glimpse of the woman beneath the smartly tailored tunic. A thin black sweater clung to her slender, long-waisted figure. Her skirt fit smoothly over gently rounded hips. With her dark hair tumbling over her shoulders, her makeup long since worn off and faint smudges darkening the skin under her eyes, she looked tired, and more vulnerable than Jack had yet seen her.

Once again the need to take her in his arms and shelter her hammered at him. She was so independent, despite her extended family. So indomitable, despite the hair-raising events she'd gone through today. Jack couldn't remember ever meeting anyone with her combination of guts and beguiling, tantalizing appeal.

When this was over, he promised himself, he'd explore the irresistable combination in greater, more intimate detail.

He tossed his suit coat over one of the rickety ladder-back chairs pulled up to the small pine table in the center of the room. His suit was considerably worse for the wear after two dive-bomb contacts with the asphalt. With a gust of relief, he dragged off his tie, undid the top few shirt buttons and rolled up the sleeves.

He turned to find Angela removing a stack of magazines from a shelflike platform built into the wall.

"Is that the bed?"

"This is the bed. You can have it, and I'll take the chair." She jerked her chin toward an overstuffed armchair piled high with fishing paraphernalia and more magazines.

"I'll take the chair."

"I've curled up in it plenty of times," she replied with a shrug, "but I'm too tired to argue. There are some blankets in those closets. If you root around, you'll probably find several bottles of Strega and some glasses."

Jack didn't have to root around. He found four dusty bottles of the potent straw-colored liqueur on the top shelf of the first cabinet, right next to an assortment of dime-store water glasses. The second closet, he noted, held a neat row of bottles containing chemicals that hadn't been purchased in any dime store. Setting the Strega and two glasses on the table, he continued his search for the blankets.

"I take it this is Uncle Guido's cabin," he commented as he carried his finds across the room.

"How did you know?"

"Do you have any other friends or relatives who keep a supply of acetone and offset ink handy?"

She bit her lower lip. "No."

"I thought he was retired."

"He is! He just prints fliers for bingo night at Saint Ignacio's. Mostly." She reached for the blankets. "I'll do these while you pour."

When both tasks were completed, Angela took advantage of the shelf/bed/sofa to rest for a few moments. Slipping off her sequin-trimmed sneakers, she sat with her back against the wall and wrapped her arms around her updrawn knees.

A glass in each hand, Jack joined her. "Scoot over." She scooted.

With his shoulders planted beside hers, he tipped his head back and closed his eyes. For the first time in almost twenty-four hours, he emptied his mind. One by one, he willed his knotted muscles to relax.

For long moments, neither one of them spoke. It was as though each of them needed time to fall back and regroup after the adrenaline-spiked day and explosive night. Time to sort through what had happened. Time to adjust to the quiet that now cradled them. Then Angela sighed and lifted her glass. Head back, she downed a healthy swallow of the pale gold liqueur.

"Drink your drink, Jack. Make your phone calls. Then we have to talk."

Weariness gave her voice a throaty rasp. The vibrant energy that was so much a part of her had dimmed. Even her hands were still, Jack saw.

With the fiery Strega burning a hole in his stomach, he located the old-fashioned black rotary-dial phone in the kitchen area and made his calls. First, to Manny Ramirez, wide-awake after his call from Ed Winters and wanting to know what the hell was going on up there. Next, to Winters himself, also wide-awake and not particularly happy about the fact that the feds were now taking over his case.

Twenty minutes later, he walked across the room and found Angela curled in a tight ball atop the cushions, sound asleep. Smiling tiredly, he covered her with the blankets. Then he ignored the overstuffed chair and nudged her gently toward the wall.

They both needed rest. Neither one of them would get any curled up in a chair. Stretching out beside her, he settled her in his arms. She made a few grumpy noises and burrowed her nose into his neck.

Just a few hours of sleep, Jack thought. That was all he needed. All his body craved. Well, not quite all. For now, though, he'd settle for a few hours of quiet with Angela in his arms.

Endless minutes later, Jack acknowledged that sleep wouldn't come as long as he was holding Angela. With every rise and fall of the soft breasts pressed against his side, her breath washed his skin. Hot. Moist. Arousing. With every twitch of her body, she brought him out of his light doze and into instant wakefulness.

He shifted slightly to find a more comfortable position on the lumpy cushions. The movement tipped her closer into his side. She muttered something unintelligible and balanced herself by flinging an arm and a leg across his body. His jaw locked as her knee landed atop his groin. Instantly hard, and now aching with a vengeance, he raised a knee to ease the tightness in his loins.

He should disengage. He should ease off the narrow plank and plant himself in the damned chair. Instead, he tucked his chin into the silky softness of her hair and waited for the dawn.

# Chapter 7

Angela woke grudgingly, as she always did.

With determined stubbornness, she hung on to the last vestiges of sleep. She ignored the tight constriction around her waist. She refused to acknowledge the faint musty odor under her nose, or even the scent of coffee drifting through the blanket she'd pulled over her head. She closed her ears to the sound of running water that had dragged her from sleep. Huddling under the covers, she fought off consciousness for a few more minutes.

She couldn't sustain the battle indefinitely. Gradually she identified the musty scent as belonging to the cushions under her nose. The tight constriction she recognized as her skirt, which had twisted around her waist. The running water...?

She frowned, trying to decide who was using the tiny bathroom her father and brother and various uncles and cousins had added to Uncle Guido's retreat last summer.

Jack.

Full awareness jolted through her.

Jack. The senator's car. Oh, God, her mother!

Thrusting her head out from under the covers, she squinted at her watch through sleep-blurred eyes.

"Yikes!"

It was almost six-thirty. She had to make arrangements for someone to pick up her boss. She had to explain to Marc Green what had happened and get someone to cover for her as the senator's driver until... Until when? Until she found out what the heck was going on.

She was fighting her way free of the tangle of blankets when Jack emerged from the bathroom.

"Sorry, did I wake you?"

"You shouldn't have let me sleep this late. You shouldn't have let me go to sleep at all until we—"

She broke off abruptly as she caught her first full look at the man. This wasn't the cool, authoritative chief financial officer who'd locked horns with her boss yesterday. This wasn't even the combination of Fred Astaire and Cary Grant who'd revved her pulse and started her heart knocking last night.

This man looked like he belonged on Tony's pit crew. Traces of a beard stubbled his cheeks and chin. His shirt was rolled up at the sleeves, showing a dusting of dark hair on his forearms. The collar gaped at the neck to reveal the strong column of his throat and curls of the same dark hair. Broad, muscular shoulders stretched the fabric at the seams.

He'd slicked his hair straight back with water, giving himself the appearance of a mature and all-too-sexy Fonz. Angela had the craziest urge to run her fingers though the black mane, just to see if it was as thick and silky as it appeared. Shoving the urge to the back of her mind where it belonged, she yanked at the covers and sat up.

"I can't believe I passed out like that."

"I can, considering everything you went through yesterday."

"Well, I've had less stressful days. Did you get any rest?" She glanced at the magazines and fishing gear still occupying the armchair. "No, I guess you didn't."

"I stretched out beside you for a few hours."

"What?"

The grin he gave her was all Fonz. Unrepentant. Unabashed. An invitation to pure trouble. "And no, I didn't get any rest."

Angela knew darn well she ought to be annoyed. She should certainly be indignant at the fact that Jack had taken it upon himself to share the narrow bed with her. Instead, all she felt was a ridiculous and overwhelming disappointment that she'd slept through the entire experience.

Next time! The swift, fierce promise darted into her mind before she could stop it. The next time she and Jack Merritt occupied the same few cubic feet of airspace, neither one of them would sleep through it!

"I found some coffee in the cupboard," he said, reclaiming her wayward attention. "I don't guarantee anything but the fact that it's hot. Do you want some to hold you over until we get breakfast?"

"Breakfast?"

"I think it's safe for us to drive back to that town we passed through last night and pick up a few essentials. We'll go as soon as you wake up...and as soon as you call your mother."

"Oh, no! Not you, too!"

"What can I say? That was the first thing Ed Winters asked about when I talked to him a while ago."

"Did he say anything else? Like who made a metal sculpture out of the senator's car?"

"No. The guys in lab coats are still going over the pieces."

With a small groan, Angela swung her legs over the edge of the narrow bed. Too late, she remembered the skirt twisted around her waist and hips. Chill morning air brushed a long length of stockinged thigh before she yanked the covers back across her lap.

Nice, Jack thought as a now familiar desire contracted his stomach muscles.

Very nice.

He turned, driven as much by the need to put some distance between himself and this sleep-tousled Angela before he did something incredibly stupid as by the recognition that she needed privacy. Scooping up the rubberized, fleece-lined anorak he'd found in one of the closets, he headed for the door.

"I'm going to take a look around outside. Get my bearings. I won't be long. If the phone rings before I get back, don't answer it. Got that?"

Angela tossed him a sort of salute. "Yes, sir! No, sir!"

Cold, damp wind skipped across the gray surface of the Chesapeake and cut into Jack's lungs as he walked the shore behind the cabin. The wind didn't, however, cut the heat in his lower body.

Shoving his hands into the parka's deep pockets, he shook his head in disgust. What in the hell was the matter with him? For the past few months, he'd walked a narrow tightrope, spending his days working the myriad problems that faced him at the hospital, and his nights and weekends up to his neck in an ever-widening investigation. For the past few days, he'd struggled to sort out the implications of Senator Claiborne's sudden summons to Washington. In the past twenty hours, he'd dodged a drive-by shooter and watched a car go up in flames.

Now, all he could think about was tumbling the senator's driver back onto a pile of musty cushions and watching her go up in flames.

Smart, Merritt. Real smart.

Manny Ramirez was on a flight to D.C. at this precise moment. Ed Winters was waiting for the agent, still not happy about the feds' involvement, but willing to co-operate. The senator would be opening his front door in a couple of hours to Manny and Ed, who'd inform him of the incident, take his statement and record his reaction.

In the midst of this tangled, dangerous situation, he had no business letting himself dwell on the long, slender curve of Angela's thigh. He sure as hell shouldn't feel this warped satisfaction at the prospect of holing up with her indefinitely.

He stopped abruptly, his shoulders hunched against the wind, as reality set in. They didn't have indefinitely. They probably didn't have more than a few hours. When Manny arrived, he'd plunge Jack back into the investigation that had consumed him these past months.

Even without Manny's presence, Jack faced another deadline. He was scheduled to testify before the congressional subcommittee at ten tomorrow morning. At this point, he had two choices. He could either appear at the hearing or tip the investigators' hands by declining to appear. In either case, he was booked on a flight

back to Atlanta tomorrow afternoon. He'd have to think
about that flight, Jack decided grimly.

If, as he suspected, he was the target of the shooting
and the car bomb, he didn't want to draw Angela any
deeper into danger than he already had. He'd have to
distance himself from her before he headed back into
civilization. If he wasn't the target, he damn sure didn't
want to leave her until he discovered who was. Jaw set,
he followed the curve of the shoreline, then circled
through the woods to familiarize himself with the terrain.

The weathered cabin sat on a spit of land that poked
out into the vast bay. Stands of tall, white-trunked oaks
and a curtain of dense undergrowth screened this stretch
of shore from the state road a quarter mile distant. Jack
trekked down the narrow, winding dirt track they'd
driven up just hours ago.

With relief, he noted that the utility wires strung
through the trees constituted the only signs of human
habitation. There were no numbers or arrows painted on
a tree trunk to indicate the dirt road led to the shanty,
no reflectors, no mailbox, no markers of any kind. Unless someone knew the cabin's exact location, it would
be difficult, if not impossible, to locate.

He retraced his steps, curious about the man who
retreated to this cabin to print fliers for bingo night at
Saint Ignacio's. Mostly. Jack wanted to meet Guido
sometime. And Tony. And Maria Paretti. When he said
as much to a scrubbed and combed Angela a few moments later, however, she shuddered.

"No, you don't! Not any time in the near future, at
least. I just talked to my mother, and she's *not* happy
about the bombing. Or about the fact that I'm secluded
at an undisclosed location with an unidentified male.

Unfortunately, she heard that part of the story before I got to her and filtered the news.''

"How?"

"How did she hear about you or how was I going to filter you out of the story?"

"How did she hear about the bombing? Ed Winters said he was going to keep it off the news as long as he could."

"I told you, my mother operates a communication net the Pentagon would kill for. Let's see if I can get this straight."

She raised a hand and ticked off the sequence. "Mother got a call from my aunt Helen, who had called to check up on her son, Leonard, who heard about the bombing from his sister Teresa, who's married to Gus."

She frowned, recounting her fingers. "Wait a minute. I think my uncle Salvatore was in the loop somewhere, too, but Mother was a bit incoherent at that point."

"Understandably so."

"I calmed her down as much as I could. Once I got her off the subject of the car bomb, though, she had a few pointed questions to ask about you. In particular, she wants to know if you have any Italian blood. You don't, do you?"

"Not a drop."

Angela nodded. "That's what I told her. She's *not* happy, Jack. To shorten her words considerably, she wants to know what in the name of the Virgin Mary and all the saints is going on. So does my father. So does Tony. So do I, incidentally."

"Get your jacket. I'll tell you what I can while we eat."

"What you can?"

Folding her arms, she refused to budge.

"That's not good enough. I want it all, Merritt. Everything. In precise detail. I'm not moving until I know why persons unnamed are trying to blow you up, and me with you. Or vice versa."

For all her flippancy, her voice had a hollow ring that made Jack's heart twist. He wanted desperately to take her in his arms. To promise her the violence was over. Since he couldn't do the one, he wouldn't let himself do the other. What he would do, though, was tell her the truth. He owed her that.

"Okay. I'll grab some coffee and we'll talk."

They sat across from each other at the scarred kitchen table. Angela propped her chin in her hands and waited while Jack skipped back through long, draining weeks.

"It started about six months ago," he said slowly, wrapping his hands around a mug emblazoned with a clipper ship in full sail. "I was working with the parents of a two-year-old hemophiliac. His name is Kevin. Kevin Crosby."

Every time Jack questioned what the hell he'd gotten himself into these past months, he thought about Kevin's mischievous grin.

"Kevin's parents are young, very young. His mother noticed that her baby bruised easily, but she didn't mention it to her doctor. She was afraid of being accused of child abuse and having her baby taken away, as she'd been removed from her own parents' house. Then Kevin crawled over a jagged plastic toy and sliced open his knee. He almost bled to death before they got him to the emergency room at Children's."

The bubbling, happy baby had captivated everyone who saw him, including Jack. But it had been his parents' desperation that got him personally involved in the child's case.

"Kevin's father works for the water department. He has a good job, but doesn't make anywhere near enough to cover the cost of his son's lifelong regimen of blood-clotting agents."

"And their insurance wouldn't cover it," Angela guessed, her voice holding only a faint trace of bitterness.

"Let's just say their insurance company took their time deciding," Jack responded.

They'd more than taken their time. They'd dragged it out, spent months wrangling with half a dozen federal agencies about the responsibility for funding the expensive treatments. Jack had finally cut through the bureaucratic red tape and located a private charity to underwrite the costs of Kevin's treatment.

"Blood-clotting agents rank right up there with growth hormones in terms of cost," he said slowly. "Given the number of patients at Children's who required these drugs, I decided to include them in a series of routine audits."

Angela leaned forward, her eyes intent. "The results weren't routine, though."

"No, they weren't. When I reviewed the preliminary data, I discovered that one of our consulting physicians had written an inordinate share of the prescriptions for Gromorphin. Sixty-seven percent, as a matter of fact."

"He sounds just like the endocrinologist Tony was referred to! Is he a quack?"

Jack took a swallow of the bitter, lukewarm coffee. "This particular physician is very highly respected at Children's. He and his wife are also two of my closest friends."

She sat back, the animation fading from her face. "Oh, no!"

"Oh, yes. When I took the findings to Philip, he admitted to accepting almost four hundred thousand dollars in kickbacks from HealthMark last year."

Compassion flooded the dark eyes across from him. Jack saw that Angela didn't need the details of the long, rainy night he'd confronted Philip Carr. She didn't need to hear a replay of his friend's anger and accusations of betrayal or, finally, his corrosive bitterness over the way he'd let himself get caught in a trap he hadn't been able to climb out of. She understood the bonds of family and friendship.

Jack rubbed the back of his neck, deliberately shoving the memory of the black, painful night he'd confronted his friend out of his mind.

"Philip cut a deal with the feds. We've both been working with the FDA and the FBI for the past four months. The investigation keeps widening at every turn, and the dollars involved are staggering. We're talking millions in fraudulent payments and unlawful subsidies."

Angela's eyes widened. "Good grief! No wonder you resisted when the senator called you to testify before his subcommittee. Why in the world didn't you tell him about this ongoing investigation?"

"Because we weren't sure why he was suddenly so interested in my audits."

"What?"

Jack set the coffee mug aside and braced himself for the storm he knew would come.

"It's entirely feasible that Senator Claiborne wanted hard, cold facts to support his medical reform legislation."

"That's exactly why he wanted them."

"Or he could've been pressured by a third party to get his hands on the audit results."

"What are you talking about?"

"You pointed out yourself that HealthMark reported more than a billion dollars in revenue from drug sales last year. That's a lot of money, Angela. It could buy a lot of influence on Capitol Hill."

Stunned, she stared at him. "Are you saying that you think HealthMark has bought the senator? Senator *Claiborne?*"

"I'm saying it's possible."

Her brows snapped together. "Watch it, Merritt. You're close to sounding like that idiot cop, Lowrey."

"It's possible, Angela."

Disbelief, denial and the beginnings of anger put spots of color high on both cheeks.

"I don't believe it! I won't believe it! Even if you showed me hard, fast proof of illegal campaign contributions or under-the-table payments disguised as honoraria, I still wouldn't believe it!"

She shoved her chair back, obviously needing maneuvering room as she underscored every passionate declaration with broad, sweeping gestures.

"I know the senator! He's devious at times, sure. He's a politician, for pity's sake! But Henry Claiborne's not on the take. He doesn't sell himself or his office."

"The stakes are too high to rule out anything or anyone."

"What about the shooting? And the car bomb? You can't possibly think the senator had anything to do with those!"

When Jack remained silent, she planted both palms on the scarred table.

"I was with you in that car, don't forget."

"I won't forget." He ground out the words. "I won't ever forget."

Their eyes clashed and held. Her chin jutted dangerously.

"I don't believe it," she repeated stubbornly.

"I didn't believe my best friend was taking kickbacks from a drug distributor, either."

That struck home. After a few moments, her angry flush subsided. She dropped back into her chair, chewing on her lower lip.

"So what do we do now?"

Jack expelled a long breath. "We get breakfast. We hope the bomb squad comes up with something. We wait for Special Agent Ramirez. He hopped a plane from Miami as soon as he learned of the bombing. Manny and Ed Winters will notify the senator about the incident last night and take his statement. In the process, they'll see if they can discover a link between his sudden interest in my audits and HealthMark."

"You won't find any link, because it doesn't exist!"

Her voice rang with certainty, but Jack caught the faint, troubled shadows in her eyes as she turned away.

They ate at a small dockside café that featured scrambled eggs, buttery grits and fried crab cakes as its only breakfast selections. Jack was quiet, thankfully, giving Angela time to absorb the implications of what he'd told her.

As she stabbed at her eggs and pushed the grits around on her plate, her absolute belief in Henry Claiborne's bedrock integrity didn't falter. She knew him. Almost as well as she knew her father and her brother or any of her uncles. He was more friend than employer, more family than friend. But worry gnawed at her, building with each passing minute.

When Jack went to pay the tab, she snuck another look at her watch. It was almost 8:15.

She had to call the senator. She had to warn him.

Jack had said that this Special Agent Ramirez and Ed Winters planned to show up at the senator's home any moment now. He wasn't there, Angela knew. He hadn't been all night.

She knew where he was, however, and she had to reach him before Ed Winters and this Special Agent Ramirez did.

"The cashier said that the gas station a few blocks down the street is also a gift shop and convenience store of sorts," Jack told her when he returned. "We can pick up what we need there."

"Good enough."

Angela drove down the single main street of the fishing village. Beyond the huddle of weathered wooden buildings, the Chesapeake rolled lines of whitecaps across its broad gray surface. A tall, white-painted lighthouse stood a lonely vigil at the end of a rocky spit.

The cold wind off the bay hit Angela in the face when she pulled up to the single pump outside the brick-fronted store and swung out of the Chevy.

"I'm going to top off the tank. I'll join you inside."

"I'll do it," Jack offered, turning up the parka's collar. "That football jacket isn't much protection from the wind."

Angela gladly handed over the nozzle. She didn't have any problem with gentlemanly instincts, as long as they didn't get in her way. In this instance, Jack's courtesy served her purpose exactly.

Letting the shop door slam shut behind her, she

ducked behind a rack of paperbacks and slipped Gus's mobile phone out of her pocket. Resolutely she squelched an uncomfortable niggle of guilt. Jack had been honest with her, as far as she knew. He'd shared information that he stressed was still very close hold. But her loyalty to her boss went far too deep for to let him become the goat in this particular sacrificial offering.

Turning her back on the man outside, she made a quick call. Her hands shook when she tucked the phone in her pocket and went to find a toothbrush and toothpaste. On the spur of the moment, she added a lipstick in a brave shade of red and some blush to the little pile of purchases.

The toothbrush and toothpaste were a matter of necessity. The makeup was for moral support. She suspected she'd need all the support she could muster when she sprang her offer on him.

# Chapter 8

The moment she and Jack returned to the cabin, Angela retreated to the bathroom with her purchases.

Stripping off the black sweater she'd slept in, she pulled on a fleecy electric-green sweatshirt emblazoned with a slightly cross-eyed seagull. Her black panty hose were replaced by thick, warm socks. The gas-station convenience store had stocked only a couple of pairs, all in men's sizes, but Angela was too grateful for the socks' warmth to mind the extra material wadding the toes of her sneakers. She dearly wanted to trade her slim black skirt for a pair of jeans, but the store's meager supplies hadn't run to that luxury.

The toothbrush and the few cosmetics she'd purchased picked her up even more than the warm, clean clothes. It was strange how much a swipe or two of lipstick and a couple of strokes of blusher could do for a woman. Armed and girded for battle, she flicked off the light and left the tiny bathroom.

Jack paced the main room, trailing the cord to the phone he held in one hand. He'd picked up some toiletries at the store, too. Shaving cream. Disposable razors. A few other items she hadn't paid attention to. Angela ran an assessing eye over his tall form. Perhaps she should delay the confrontation between them until after he had a chance to put the shaving cream and a razor to use. It might be smarter to wait until the smooth, civilized Jack Merritt reemerged.

This one was too rugged-looking. Too tough and uncompromising. The dark stubble on his chin and cheeks emphasized a square, firm jaw. His muscles bunched under the thick cable-knit fisherman's sweater he'd purchased at a wildly exorbitant price, much to the store owner's delight. His long legs ate up the floor as he traced a path from the table to the kitchen counter, whipping the cord along behind him.

His dark brows slashed, he listened to the speaker at the other end of the line. Then he hung up with a terse ''I'll get back to you'' and turned to face her. From his tight, flat expression, Angela knew she couldn't delay the inevitable any longer.

''Problems?'' she inquired. ''Other than a melted car and drive-by shooter, I mean?''

''That was Manny Ramirez. They just left the senator's house.''

Angela hid her swift stab of relief. Her boss had returned home in time!

His gray eyes as hard and flat as tempered steel, Jack added a kicker. ''They came away with a written authorization to examine the senator's personal bank accounts and personal financial records.''

''Good.''

''Good?'' he echoed softly. Dangerously. ''You don't sound very surprised, Angela.''

''I'm not,'' she said as steadily as she could.

''Why not?''

''Because I called him earlier, at the convenience store. While you were pumping gas.''

Anger knifed through Jack like a sharp, serrated blade. He'd followed his instincts. He'd told Angela more than he probably should have. He couldn't believe he'd been so wrong about her, or that she'd flung his confidences back in his face.

As swiftly as his anger and bitter frustration rose, Jack fought to master it. He'd been up to his neck in this morass for the past four months, he reminded himself savagely. Angela had been plunged into it less than twenty-four hours ago. He couldn't expect her to abandon her passionate belief in her boss so swiftly. Common sense told him she needed more convincing. Logic dictated that he give her more time.

Still, he knew damn well that accusation was written all across his face when Angela lifted her chin and met his stare head-on.

''I didn't tell the senator about the Chrysler going up in smoke,'' she told him, her eyes flashing. ''Or about the details of the investigation. I didn't even mention Gromorphin or HealthMark.''

''Then what the hell *did* you tell him?''

''That he could trust you. And Ed Winters.''

The sweeping simplicity of her declaration rocked Jack back on his heels. He was still trying to absorb it when she launched into an impassioned explanation.

''I know the senator, Jack. Marc Green told you that I serve as more than just his driver. It's true. We've grown close these past three years, as close as family.

He's trusted me with personal information he hasn't shared with the rest of his staff.''

"And?"

"And I convinced him to share that information with you."

"Why?"

"I told you, he trusts me." She folded her arms across the cockeyed seagull on her chest and glared at him. "And I trust you."

Her belligerence took the last of Jack's anger.

"You may be part of a flawed system," she continued grudgingly, "but at least you're trying to do something about it. You're trying to fix it. We're on the same side, Jack. So is the senator."

He rubbed the back of his neck, thinking hard. He'd been up to his ass in suspicions and doubts and conspiracies for so long that Angela's behind-the-scenes machinations and the senator's willingness to cooperate seemed too good to be true.

They *were* too good to be true, he realized. True, she'd apparently engineered Claiborne's full cooperation. And, true, she'd been up-front about it. But Angela Paretti's loyalty to family and friends wouldn't let her throw her boss to the wolves, not even to a wolf she supposedly trusted. Hooking one of the kitchen chairs, Jack yanked it around and pointed to the seat.

"Sit down. I want to go over this one more time. Just to make sure I understand it."

Angela perched on the edge of the seat, her hands tucked under her thighs. Jack pulled out the other chair and straddled it.

"The senator's agreed to give us full access to his personal financial records, is that correct?"

"Correct."

"Why?"

"Because he doesn't have anything to hide from special investigators."

"And in exchange?"

Her eyes glinted. "In exchange, you keep the inquiry quiet, Jack. Very quiet. No leaks to the media. No disclosures to his staff. In this town, a man's guilty long before he even knows the charges against him."

"I can't promise that, Angela. If the senator's linked to HealthMark in any illegal way—"

"He isn't."

"If he is, he'll face possible prosecution alongside the others caught in this mess."

"Senator Claiborne's only connection to HealthMark is the fact that they're as nervous about his reform legislation as the rest of the medical community. He's going to help you make them even more nervous."

For the first time since they'd returned to the cabin, she threw Jack one of those grins that hit him like a fist to the solar plexus. It was all Angela, sparkling and vibrant and full of glinting challenge.

"And when this investigation's over, *you're* going to give Senator Henry Claiborne full credit for helping uncover sweeping fraud and corruption in a system that badly needs reform."

Jack sat back, shaking his head. "I don't believe this. An hour ago you were ready to take my head off for even suggesting your boss could be involved with HealthMark. Now you've found a way to make him the hero of the entire investigation."

"That's how it goes in politics or at the racetrack, big guy. You take advantage of every opening in the pack, no matter how small, and surge into the lead."

She hunched her shoulders, excitement and anticipation radiating from her in almost palpable waves. Jack felt her energy arc through the air. It formed a bridge between them. Healed the hurt caused by his knifing suspicion and her divided loyalties. Bonded them together, even more closely than they'd bonded during those few moments on the Fourteenth Street Bridge.

Suddenly, they shared the satisfaction of being on the same team, of working together, as they had last night. Only this time, they were equals, instead of instructor and driver-in-training.

"What do we do now?" she asked with a touch of impatience.

He glanced at his watch. "The banks don't open until ten. It'll take Manny some time to gather the senator's financial records. I figure we've got three hours, four max. Then he'll arrive at our front door with a vanload of boxes, several computers and document scanners, a fax machine and a team of auditors for me to oversee. He seems to think I have special powers when it comes to crunching numbers," Jack added.

"Do you?"

"Yes." He held up a palm. "I know, I know. You consider number crunchers among the lower life-forms that inhabit the planet. But you have to admit we're at least a half step up from the Browsers of the world."

"Well..." She examined the tips of her sneakers. "I've been thinking about what you said on the bridge. It's possible, just possible, you understand, that some of you might be human after all."

"Careful, Paretti. You're starting to sound a lot like that idiot cop, Lowrey."

The hint of laughter in his voice brought her head up. When she caught the glint in his gray eyes, Angela's heart thumped painfully.

How did he do that? she wondered. How in the world did this exasperating man propel her from anger to excitement to this tingling sense of awareness so quickly, so effortlessly? Granted, she tended to be a bit emotional at times. True, she believed in living every minute of life to the fullest. But she felt as though she'd been plunging down the slopes and charging up the peaks of a huge, continuous roller coaster since the moment she met Jack Merritt. Even for her, the pace was breathtaking.

So was the expression on his face at this particular moment. Angela's heart gave another thump.

"You know," he said conversationally, "we never finished our experiment."

"What experiment?"

He pushed himself off the chair. "We were trying another kiss, remember? With your eyes closed. To see if I could prove just how human I can be at times."

She scrambled to her feet. "I remember. I also remember that every time we get close to each other, something seems to explode."

His smile started in his eyes and worked its way down to his mouth. Fascinated, Angela followed its progress. He had a beautiful mouth, she thought. Firm. Well shaped. Just right for kissing and being kissed.

"If I don't get close to you soon," he murmured, "something's definitely going to explode."

He a took a step toward her. Angela's arms shot out. "Wait!"

"I've been waiting. I'm still waiting. I don't want to wait any longer."

Palms flat against his chest, she held him off. Or herself off. At this point, she wasn't quite sure.

"Let's talk about this, Jack."

"Is that what you really want to do? Talk?"

He must have read the answer in her eyes.

"We've got three, maybe four hours." He reached out to brush a wayward strand of hair from her forehead. "We'll talk later."

His touch was so gentle, so electric, that her elbows bent. And her willpower. Swallowing, Angela made a last valiant effort to inject some stability into a situation that was fast getting out of control.

"This isn't smart. We hardly know each other."

His nose brushed the tip of hers. "True. But I went past smart when I donned that silly top hat last night. And I can't think of a better way for us to get to know each other."

He had to remind her of that hat! He'd looked so handsome in it. So smooth and debonair.

Last night, his bristles hadn't scraped her chin the way they did now. The collar of his starched white shirt hadn't been scrunched up on one side and down on the other. Given the choice, though, Angela knew she'd rather feel the bristles than gawk up at a Cary Grant look-alike.

This Jack was so real to her. So close and warm and real. Suddenly, desperately, she wanted the taste of his mouth on hers. Bending her elbows a few more degrees, she rose up on tiptoe.

"Maybe if we do this very slowly and very carefully," she whispered, "the roof won't blow off or the windows shatter."

"I'm all for slowly," he said. "Very slowly."

He didn't crowd her. Didn't close the small space between them. Neither did she.

His head angled.

Hers tilted.

**GAME CARD 1**

# Win $ TRIPLE LUCKY Lotto

## Up To $1,000,000

Scratch off Gold Panel on tickets 1-7 until at least 5 (hearts) are revealed on one ticket. Doing so makes you eligible for a chance to win one of the following prizes: Grand Prize, $1,000,000.00; 1st Prize, $50,000.00; 2nd Prize, $10,000.00; 3rd Prize, $5,000.00; 4th Prize, $1,000.00; 5th Prize, $250.00; 6th Prize, $10.00.

**GAME CARD 4**

# Win $ TRIPLE LUCKY Lotto

## Up To $1,000,000

Scratch off Gold Panel on tickets 1-7 until at least 5 (hearts) are revealed on one ticket. Doing so makes you eligible for a chance to win one of the following prizes: Grand Prize, $1,000,000.00; 1st Prize, $50,000.00; 2nd Prize, $10,000.00; 3rd Prize, $5,000.00; 4th Prize, $1,000.00; 5th Prize, $250.00; 6th Prize, $10.00.

**GAME CARD 7**

# Win $ TRIPLE LUCKY Lotto

## Up To $1,000,000

Scratch off Gold Panel on tickets 1-7 until at least 5 (hearts) are revealed on one ticket. Doing so makes you eligible for a chance to win one of the following prizes: Grand Prize, $1,000,000.00; 1st Prize, $50,000.00; 2nd Prize, $10,000.00; 3rd Prize, $5,000.00; 4th Prize, $1,000.00; 5th Prize, $250.00; 6th Prize, $10.00.

# Win $ TRIPLE LUCKY Lotto

## Up To $1,000,000

Scratch off Gold Panel on tickets 1-7 until at least 5 (hearts) are revealed on one ticket. Doing so makes you eligible for a chance to win one of the following prizes: Grand Prize, $1,000,000.00; 1st Prize, $50,000.00; 2nd Prize, $10,000.00; 3rd Prize, $5,000.00; 4th Prize, $1,000.00; 5th Prize, $250.00; 6th Prize, $10.00.

ALL PRIZES GUARANTEED TO BE AWARDED

# Win $ TRIPLE LUCKY Lotto

## Up To $1,000,000

Scratch off Gold Panel on tickets 1-7 until at least 5 (hearts) are revealed on one ticket. Doing so makes you eligible for a chance to win one of the following prizes: Grand Prize, $1,000,000.00; 1st Prize, $50,000.00; 2nd Prize, $10,000.00; 3rd Prize, $5,000.00; 4th Prize, $1,000.00; 5th Prize, $250.00; 6th Prize, $10.00.

ALL PRIZES GUARANTEED TO BE AWARDED

# Win $ TRIPLE LUCKY Lotto

## For FREE BOOKS

Scratch off the Gold Panel. You will receive one FREE BOOK for each ★ that appears. See the back of this Game Card for details.

RETURN ALL 9 GAME CARDS INTACT

Dear Reader,

**YOU MAY BE A MAILBOX AWAY FROM BEING OUR NEW MILLION $$ WINNER!**

Scratch off the gold on Game Cards 1-7 to automatically qualify for a chance to win a cash prize of up to $1 Million in lifetime cash! Do the same on Game Cards 8 & 9 to automatically get free books and a free surprise gift -- and to try Silhouette's no-risk Reader Service. It's a delightful way to get our best novels each month -- at discount -- with no obligation to buy, ever. Here's how it works, satisfaction fully guaranteed:

After receiving your free books, if you don't want any more, just write "cancel" on the accompanying statement, and return it to us. If you do not cancel, each month we'll send you 6 additional novels to read and enjoy & bill you just $3.34 each plus 25¢ delivery per book and applicable sales tax, if any.* That's the complete price, and -- compared to cover prices of $3.99 each -- quite a bargain!

You may cancel at any time, but if you choose to continue, every month we'll send you 6 more books, which you may either purchase at the discount price...or return to us and cancel your subscription.

**P.S. Don't Forget to include your Bonus Token.**

**SEE BACK OF BOOK FOR SWEEPSTAKES DETAILS. ENTER TODAY, AND...** *Good Luck!*

His kiss was light. Slow. Careful. Too careful, Angela decided with a shiver of need. She drew back, her head cocked, in a listening mode.

"I don't hear anything."

He explored the skin at the side of her neck. "No ticking time bombs?"

"No." She hunched a shoulder as his breath warmed her ear.

"No rumblings to signify an imminent earthquake?"

"Well…maybe a few small tremors."

He lifted his head. "Only a few small tremors? Let's see if we can do better than that."

Tossing aside the last of her reservations, Angela went into his arms. They had three, maybe four hours alone together. After that, the outside world would once again intrude. For these three hours, though, there was just her and Jack and this sudden, leaping hunger she saw in his face and felt deep in her bones.

Her head went back. When his came down, Angela closed her eyes. A small, detached part of her remained on full alert, fully expecting disaster to strike. One second slipped by. Two. The cabin walls didn't implode. The roof stayed intact. She went boneless with relief and gave herself up to his kiss.

As they had last night, her toes curled in her sneakers. As she had last night, she threaded her fingers through the springy hair at the back of his neck. His whiskers scraped her chin, adding an unexpected sting to the pleasure that zinged through her veins.

For all the icy control she'd seen Jack exercise at various times in the past twenty-odd hours, he couldn't disguise his body's reaction to its contact with hers. His muscles tensed. His arms tightened around her waist. His breath grew as short and ragged as hers. Then he widened his stance, canting her into the cradle of his hips.

Angela's eyes flew open.

She no longer had any doubts. This man was most definitely human. If the rock-solid hardness of his lower body hadn't convinced her, the heat singeing his face certainly would have. She was trying to command her wobbly legs to step back, away from the intimate contact, when Jack tugged her arms from around his neck.

"I don't think I can take any more experimentation," he muttered.

"We can try another test-drive later," she said lightly, hiding her own shakiness in the flippant reply. "With *your* eyes closed this time. Just to see if it makes a difference, you understand."

"Oh, no, sweetheart. No more tests or trials. The next time's for real."

Her stomach did a double back flip at the steely promise in his eyes.

"You pick the time," Jack said softly. "And the place."

*Now!* she wanted to cry. *Here!*

Instead, she backed away. It was too soon. She wasn't ready. There were too many unresolved issues between them. She couldn't give in to this wild, insistent clamoring in her heart.

"I'll, uh, let you know," she got out.

"You do that," he replied, his smile tipping into a heady, intoxicating grin. "Just be prepared for—"

He broke off, his head snapping up.

"What?" Angela demanded.

"I thought I heard something."

She moaned. "I knew it! I knew disaster would strike the minute we kissed!"

"Quiet!"

His every sense straining, Jack listened intently. There it was again. A faint hum. A car engine, he decided. Or a plane.

Instincts, honed to a razor's sharpness by his years on the SEAL team, took over. Without thinking, his mind clicked to the three *R*s…the three basic tasks that had kept him and his fellow team members alive in more situations than he wanted to remember.

Reconnoiter.

Recognize.

Remove.

The team hadn't included retreat in their lexicon.

Jack had already accomplished the first *R*. Before Angela woke up this morning, he'd inventoried the contents of the cabin's interior for possible offensive and defensive weapons. His long walk had given him a fix on the surrounding terrain.

His task now was to identify whether friend or foe approached. If foe, he'd remove the threat.

"Get your coat!"

While Angela scrambled for the football jacket she'd looped over the back of a kitchen chair, Jack crossed the cabin in three swift strides. Yanking open the pine cabinets, he pocketed two plastic bottles of Uncle Guido's chemicals. Then he swooped up the collection of small, sharp carving knives he'd discovered in a box beside a half-finished wooden duck. Lastly he grabbed the cellular phone that had come with Gus's Chevy. Shoving the phone into Angela's hand, he hustled her out the door.

The sound carried clearly on the cold, thin air. Unmistakably a car. Jack could hear the crunch of tires as they traveled the winding dirt track to the cabin. He spun Angela around, pointing her at the woods on the north side of the cabin.

"Keep under cover. Head north toward the village, and don't use the phone unless you have to. If we're dealing with unfriendlies here, I don't want them to get a lock on you. If we're not, I'll come after you."

"Wait a minute! Where are you going?"

"Move it, Angela! Now!"

She threw him a glare that was part worry, part confusion, and all determination.

"I can help."

"I don't have time to argue, and I don't want to risk both our lives by worrying about you blundering around behind me. Move it!"

Her eyes flashed but, thankfully, she moved it. Jack didn't wait for the trees to swallow her up. He couldn't. Their unannounced visitor was closer now. He had to get himself in position, and fast.

He raced for the spot he'd picked out earlier this morning. Screened by the white-barked oaks and thick underbrush, it commanded a good view of the clearing in front of the cabin and an even better one of the last curve of the dirt lane. He dived behind the prickly curtain of brush mere seconds before a low-slung, cherry-red sports car nosed around the bend.

He couldn't see enough of the driver through the Corvette's tinted windows to identify him. He waited, his pulse slowing to the curious calm that had always settled over him just before the team hit the beach or the chutes. His fingers curved around the wooden shaft of the largest carving knife.

The Corvette pulled up alongside Gus's Chevy.

Jack's jaw clenched as questions tumbled through his mind. Logic told him that the individual or individuals who planted the bomb last night wouldn't drive right up to the cabin in broad daylight, but he wasn't operating on logic at this moment.

The Corvette's door opened. A lone individual emerged. Mirrored sunglasses and the upturned collar of his leather bomber jacket disguised his features, but Jack saw enough to know that he didn't recognize this character as friend.

Which meant he had to be considered foe.

Reversing the knife, he slid the blade down until he gripped it at the tip. At this distance, he couldn't miss.

The stranger took two steps toward the cabin. Jack noted the slight drag to his left leg before rapping out a low, flat order.

"Hold it right there, pal."

The other man froze.

"I want to see your hands. Both hands. Now!"

The stranger's hands went up. Slowly. Just as slowly, he turned around.

Jack kept the sun at his back and the shield of trees in front. "Who are you?"

"Who wants to know?"

Before either man got an answer to his question, the sound of someone crashing out of the brush on the far side of the clearing spun them both around. The unidentified visitor dropped into an instinctive crouch and Jack's arm came straight back.

He gave a short, vicious curse as Angela raced right into his trajectory. With an inarticulate cry, she launched herself at the stranger.

# Chapter 9

By the time Jack reached the entangled pair, he'd already realized that Angela wasn't struggling in the stranger's arms. Nor was she trying to drag him down, as she'd done to Jack on the Fourteenth Street Bridge. Just the opposite, in fact. She'd thrown both arms around his neck and was now embracing him with as much fervor as he embraced her with.

All right. Okay. Jack could handle the sight of Angela hugging this character and planting wet, smacking kisses on his cheek.

Maybe.

His jaw locked tight, he waited for the demonstration to end. When Angela finally turned, a joyful smile lit her face.

"This is my brother, Tony. Tony, this is Jack Merritt."

At that point, Jack didn't need her breathless introduction. With brother and sister now standing side by side, the family resemblance was unmistakable. Both Angela and Tony Paretti possessed the same dark, curly hair. The same olive-tinted skin. The same wide, generous mouth and pointed chin.

But there the resemblance ended. Where Angela's slender figure curved in exactly the right places, her brother was built along more solid, powerful lines. His leather jacket emphasized muscled shoulders. Well-worn jeans hugged corded thighs. If Tony had sustained much tissue damage in the crash that almost took his life three years ago, he'd worked hard to overcome it. The only visible signs of his near-fatal accident were his limp and the network of scars that ran down one side of his throat and disappeared in the collar of his jacket.

With his free hand, Tony peeled off his sunglasses. Eyes the same shade of liquid brown as Angela's raked Jack from head to toe. They snagged on the knife still held in Jack's hand for a moment, then sliced to his face.

"So you're Merritt."

Angela's smile took a nosedive at the implacable you've-just-met-your-doom note in her brother's voice. She'd obviously heard that tone before.

"I'm Merritt," he replied, meeting the hostile gaze head-on.

"I heard about you from Ed Winters. And from Gus. You and I are going to have a little talk before you leave Washington, *pal.*"

"Fine by me."

With a sigh of exasperation, Angela realized that the past few adrenaline-pumping moments must have maxed out Jack's macho quotient. Tony's generally stayed maxed out. Valiantly she threw herself into the widening breach.

"How did you know where we were?" she asked, twisting out of her brother's hold.

"How do you think?" His terse reply promised a no-holds-barred brother-and-sister chat later.

Angela groaned. "Mother."

"Right the first time."

"She activated the worldwide net?"

Her brother's tight expression eased a fraction. "By a process of elimination, she discovered that you weren't staying with any relatives, friends or business acquaintances, and that you weren't at any of the hotels listed in the D.C. or Maryland directories. I had a suspicion you might head here, and decided to check it out."

"Does anyone else know we're here?" Jack asked sharply.

Tony's hostile gaze slewed to him. "No."

"Any chance you were followed?"

His mouth curled. "No. But in any case, it's a moot point. I'm taking my sister out of here. Now. You can find yourself another hole to burrow into."

"Wait a minute!"

Tony might have ignored Angela's protest, but he couldn't ignore the way Jack placed himself squarely in front of them. The two men looked each other up and down, and then her brother issued the challenge he'd obviously been itching to get out.

"You got any objections, Merritt?"

"I might, but whether Angela goes or stays is her choice."

The deliberate drawl narrowed Tony's eyes. "Not this time."

"Yes, this time," she insisted, reclaiming his attention with a yank on his sleeve. "You don't know what's involved here. I do."

"So tell me."

She shot Jack a quick glance. His still, watchful eyes telegraphed no permission to share what he'd told her about the investigation. Nor did they withhold it. The decision was hers, just as the decision to call the senator earlier had been hers.

Angela hesitated, as torn now as she'd been when she made the call. She hadn't betrayed Jack's confidences then. She couldn't now. But holding back wrenched something deep and fundamental inside her.

She'd always told Tony everything. Well, almost everything. Every childish dream. Every girlhood crush. She'd shared the joys and disappointments in her life, and the dangerous excitement of his. He'd guided her, encouraged her, protected her...until she made it clear she didn't want or need big brother's protection any longer.

Unable to give him the explanation he demanded, Angela took refuge in a cowardly delaying tactic.

"Why don't we go inside? Get out of the cold?"

The moment the door shut behind them, she realized her mistake. As a kid, Tony had spent as many weekends out at the shanty as she had. He knew exactly what the cabin offered in terms of sleeping accommodations. His gaze zeroed in on the armchair, still littered with Uncle Guido's fishing gear and a collection of racing magazines, then whipped to the narrow bed. That, unfortunately, still carried the evidence of its recent occupancy.

His hands curled into fists. He turned to face Jack, who met his accusing stare head-on.

She didn't need this, Angela thought. With everything else that had happened to her in the past twenty-four hours, she didn't need the brother she loved coming to blows with the man she— Her racing thoughts stumbled to a halt. The man she what?

She'd have to figure out that one later. Right now, though, she'd better defuse the situation before Uncle Guido's cabin went the way of the Chrysler.

"You taught me to take care of myself, Tony," she said, planting herself firmly between the two men. "You also taught me to make my own decisions. Whatever happened or didn't happen here last night is my business."

He didn't like it. She could see it in his face and in the way he rolled his shoulders back, like a bull terrier scenting a rat.

Jack didn't like it, either. His jaw squaring, he edged Angela to one side and faced her brother.

"Whatever happened or didn't happen here last night is my business, too. Do you have a problem with that, Paretti?"

"I might," Tony drawled, in deliberate imitation of Jack's accent. "I just might."

The testosterone was so thick, it could have been cut with a knife. An apt metaphor, Angela thought in disgust.

"I give up!" she told the two men. "Go ahead, pound each other into the floor, if it'll make you both feel better. Just don't expect me to stand here and watch."

She stomped to the front door. "And don't expect me to dispense tea and Band-Aids when you two get through. I'm going for a walk!"

The door banged shut behind her. In the ensuing silence, neither man moved.

As he faced Paretti, Jack fought to bring the primitive combativeness pulsing through his veins under control. He knew damn well his own bristling hostility stemmed as much from long, tense weeks with the investigation team as from the gut-twisting few moments he'd just experienced. He also knew that his next move could make a serious difference to where he and Angela went from here.

"I don't know about dispensing tea," he said, measuring each word with care, "but I found some coffee in the cupboard."

For several long seconds, Paretti seemed poised to reject the offer of a temporary truce. His shoulders rolled once more, and his dark eyes cut like lasers across the still, unmoving air.

"Forget the coffee," he growled at last. "Uncle Guido keeps a supply of Strega on hand for emergencies. I think this qualifies."

Jack thought so, too.

He'd drunk enough of the fiery liqueur last night to refrain from downing it in a couple of large swallows, as Tony did. Even with his more cautious approach, however, the pale liquid burned a track down the back of his throat. When it engaged in mortal combat with the grits and greasy crab cakes Jack had eaten for breakfast, a light sweat broke out on his brow.

Pulling out a chair, Tony planted himself at the table. "All right, Merritt. I want to know what's going on."

Jack took the opposite chair. "I can't tell you. Not everything."

"Give me the shortened version, then," he said sardonically. "One I can give my mother. You better know that I'm under orders not to return to Baltimore without Angela...or a damned convincing explanation of why she's not with me.''

When Jack hesitated, Paretti leaned forward, all trace of mockery gone. His face was serious. Dead serious.

"Is someone after my sister?"

"It's possible the shooting on the bridge was a random act of violence," Jack said slowly. "Angela got a glimpse of the driver, enough to do a composite. It's also possible that the car bomb was an attempt to eliminate her as a witness."

"Possible, but not probable?"

"Possible enough that I wanted to get her to a safe place while the police checked it out."

"This seclusion was your idea?"

"That's right."

As Tony weighed the reply, the lambent hostility slowly drained from his face. He poured himself another shot of potent liqueur. When he looked up again, his eyes held a speculative look.

"Just how long have you known my sister?"

"I met her yesterday, when she picked me up at the airport."

"Yesterday, huh?"

His glance dropped. Pale gold liquid coated the sides of the water glass as he tipped it from side to side.

"It happens like that sometimes," he murmured, half to himself.

From the look on Paretti's face, Jack guessed it had happened to him, too. But apparently Angela's brother wasn't any more sure what to do about it than she was. With a little shake of his head, Tony returned to the urgent matter that had brought him to the cabin.

"All right. We agree that it's possible Angela's the

target of these attacks. If she is, I'll know soon enough. If she's not, we'll know who is."

Jack jerked up straight. "How the hell will you know that?"

A small, tight smile flitted across Tony's face. "One of our relatives, currently retired, still maintains a few useful contacts on the streets."

"Uncle Guido?"

"You know about him, do you?"

Jack nodded, satisfaction spearing through him at the idea of the former counterfeiter using his network of accomplices and acquaintances to complement the efforts of the police.

"I know enough about Uncle Guido to want to meet him before I leave Washington."

"I think we can arrange that," Tony replied dryly. "Unless you also want to meet my mother, though, and real soon, you'd better tell me what you really think is going on."

Jack drew in a slow breath. He'd laid everything out for Angela. He couldn't do the same for her brother, not in specific detail.

"All I can tell you is that I'm involved in an investigation into possible fraud and corruption by a major pharmaceutical distributor. The corporation in question doesn't know about the investigation, or how much we've uncovered about their activities. But they're nervous. Very nervous."

"Even more nervous, now that you're about to testify before a congressional subcommittee looking into medical reform legislation," Tony guessed shrewdly.

"Possibly."

He hooked a brow. "That's why you're here, isn't it? To testify?"

"That's the reason the senator gave for his 'invitation.'"

"What other reason could he have for hauling you up to D.C.?"

"I've been asking myself that, too."

It took only a few seconds for Tony to grasp the implications of Jack's neutral response, and even less time to reject it.

"If you think Henry Claiborne's somehow involved in this fraud and corruption you talked about, you're wrong. Flat wrong. I don't believe it. You could produce a mountain of evidence, and I still wouldn't believe it. Neither would my sister."

"So she informed me."

Paretti leaned forward, his face carved in hard, unyielding angles. "In case you haven't noticed, Merritt, Angela doesn't do anything by halves. Those she loves, she loves wholly and unconditionally. I don't know what's happening or not happening between the two of you, but I'll tell you this. She'll never forgive you if you drag the senator's name into the dirt."

"Senator Claiborne's cooperating in the investigation," Jack replied evenly, but Tony's warning was still echoing in his mind when Angela returned a little while later.

The cold wind had whipped flags of color into her cheeks and tossed her hair all over her head. In her grabbag ensemble of green sweatshirt, navy-and-tan football jacket, black skirt and gray athletic socks, she looked like a garage-sale junkie.

She stopped just inside the door, eyeing the dusty green bottle on the table with a lift of one brow.

"What is this, a change in tactics? Instead of beating

each other into the ground, you're going to see who can drink who under the table?''

Tony shoved back his chair. ''The way I see it, I have two choices. I either bring you back to Baltimore with me, or I fortify myself with enough Strega to explain to Mom why I didn't.''

''Then you'd better take the bottle with you,'' she retorted.

Crossing to her side, Tony curled a knuckle under her chin and tilted her face to his.

''I don't like this,'' he said quietly. ''I don't like leaving you here, and I don't like leaving with so many unanswered questions.''

She curled her hand over his. ''I know, Tony. But I have to stay until those questions get answered. I owe the senator that much. We both do.''

''Yeah.'' He brushed a kiss across her cheek. ''Be careful, brat.''

''I will.''

Pulling his sunglasses out of his pocket, he tossed a curt order over his shoulder. ''Walk outside with me, Merritt. I've got a few last words of advice for you that my sister doesn't need to hear.''

Half-amused, wholly embarrassed, Angela didn't even try to protest. Folding her arms, she leaned against the door frame and watched the two men walk to the bright red Corvette. Tony's mirrored glasses and up-turned collar hid most of his expression from Angela. But there was no way she could miss the glint of sunlight on blue steel as he pulled a small snub-nosed revolver from his pocket and passed it to Jack.

Nor did she miss Jack's cool confidence as he thumbed open the cylinder, examined its contents and snapped it back into place. After pocketing the weapon, he exchanged a few short sentences with Tony. A few moments later, the red Corvette headed down the narrow dirt track.

Feeling disconcerted and off balance after her brother's unexpected visit, Angela accompanied Jack back into the cabin. While he locked the door and unloaded an assortment of bottles and weapons from his pockets, she decided she'd better get busy, as well.

Her most pressing task was to remove all evidence of the bed's double occupancy before other visitors arrived—her mother, for instance. Despite Tony's assurances that he'd do his best, Angela knew darn well that even he couldn't keep Maria Paretti from descending on the cabin if she decided to provide personal protection for her chick.

Tugging one of the blankets from the narrow shelf, she hooked an edge under her chin and stretched to catch its corners. Of their own volition, her eyes lingered on the bed. She couldn't quite believe that she and Jack had shared that small space last night. Or that she'd slept through the entire experience. The next time, though... Her pulse skittering wildly, she clutched the half-folded blanket to her chest.

The next time, she'd promised herself, she'd be awake.

The next time, Jack had said, would be for real.

"Need some help?"

Angela jumped half out of her sneakers. She'd been so absorbed in contemplating that shimmering, ephemeral next time that she hadn't even heard his approach. Her cheeks warming, she turned and handed him the ends of the blanket.

"Yes, thanks. I thought I'd better straighten up. Just in case..."

"Just in case more of your family members arrive?" he asked, his eyes gleaming as he matched his corners to the ones in her hand. "Or in case they jump to more conclusions about last night?"

"Both," she admitted, her face heating even more.

Turning away, she executed a somewhat sloppy fold and fumbled for the corners of the second blanket. This was ridiculous. Why in the world should this simple, shared task send shivers coursing through her? Why should she blush like a schoolgirl at the thought of these rough wool blankets wrapped around her and Jack last night?

Nothing had happened! Nothing, darn it.

The next time, though...

She had no business thinking about a next time, she told herself sternly. Not until this business with the senator was resolved. Not until she'd won Jack's support for his proposed legislation. And certainly not until the police discovered who was behind these attacks.

It was stupid...dangerous...*crazy*...to dwell on the way her mouth had molded his in those breathless moments before Tony's arrival. Or the way Jack's body had hardened against hers. Or how much she wanted the next time to be right here, and right now.

They had only a few hours, she reminded herself. Just a few more hours, according to Jack's estimate, until this special agent arrived or they left to go meet him. Angela wasn't about to let this crazy, swirling need inside her push her into something she wasn't quite ready for.

"You do this," she said gruffly, thrusting the blanket into Jack's hands. "I'll pick up the rest of our things."

Breathing deeply to drag some air into her lungs, she scooped up the discarded sweater she'd tossed over the back of the big, cluttered armchair. With a quick roll, she tucked the black sweater into her purse. Since she'd have to wear the tunic when she returned to civilization, it received better treatment.

Smoothing a hand down its length to erase the wrinkles, she felt a bulge in one of the pockets. Frowning, she reached inside and closed her fingers around a wad of tissue. Something sharp sliced into her skin.

Her palm stinging, she withdrew her hand to find a piece of glass embedded deep in the heel of her hand. Before she could dig it out, blood welled around the small wound and ran down her wrist.

"Great," she muttered, dropping the jacket to dab at the blood with the wadded tissue.

At her muted exclamation, Jack tossed the blanket down and strode to her side.

"What happened?"

"I forgot about the sliver of glass I dug out of your suit collar yesterday. The thing was in my pocket. Now it's in my hand."

"Here, let me."

He took her hand and turned it palm up to the light streaming in through the windows. His touch gentle, he blotted the seeping blood.

"Looks like it's in pretty deep. Come into the bathroom. We'll wash the blood away and do an FOE."

"What's an FOE?" she asked suspiciously.

"Foreign Object Extraction," he translated, holding her hand under a slow trickle of cold water. "Relax. I used to be a navy corpsman, remember? I've pulled all kinds of foreign bodies out of sailors and marines, some they wanted to get rid of, some they didn't."

"Oh, that's comforting."

Grinning, he bent to examine the embedded sliver. Angela's shoulders brushed his as she angled to give him more room at the tiny sink.

"Hmmm."

"Hmmm? That's the best you can do? Just hmmm?"

"You don't happen to have any tweezers in your purse, do you?"

"No. Everything else but," she admitted, flinching a little at his gentle, exploratory squeeze. "Try the medicine cabinet. Uncle Guido laid in a store of emergency supplies after one of my cousins' kids caught his brother on the end of a fishhook."

Jack's search of the mirrored cabinet above the sink turned up a half-used tube of antiseptic cream, a rusted tin of Band-Aids and an eyedropper, but no tweezers. Setting the cream and Band-Aids on the edge of the sink, he closed the mirror and tilted Angela's hand to the light above it.

"I'll have to dig it out. Hold still."

She held still. He bent closer, steadying her hand with his as his fingers got a tentative grip on the slippery protruding edge. She breathed a sigh of relief as it came out cleanly. Jack dropped the glass onto the sink's rim and folded a washcloth over the fresh welling of blood.

"Sit down. The bleeding should slow in a minute or two, then we'll bandage you up."

While Angela lowered the toilet lid and sat sideways on the only seat in the tiny bathroom, Jack twisted off the cap on the tube of antiseptic, then popped open the tin box and extracted some Band-Aids.

"Let's see how you're doing," he said a few moments later.

She was doing fine...until he hunkered down on one

heel beside her. Suddenly, the minuscule bathroom shrank to even smaller dimensions. He nudged her knees aside with his hips, and Angela found herself wedged between the solid, rough-planed pine wall and Jack's equally solid frame.

She scooted over as far as she could to make room for him. Too late, she saw that the movement had parted the side slit in her skirt all the way up her thigh. Her bare thigh. She wiggled and reached across her lap with the opposite hand to draw her skirt closed.

"Hold still," he commanded again.

Right. Uh-huh. She was supposed to hold still, with his warm breath washing her hand *and* her thigh? With his body caging hers? With her heart pounding out this slow, unsteady rhythm?

She slumped against the wall, repeating the litany she'd chanted just moments ago in the other room. This was stupid. Dangerous. Crazy! She shouldn't ache to curl the fingers of her free hand in Jack's dark hair. She shouldn't want to slide off the john and into the vee between his legs.

She shouldn't, but she did. More than she could ever remember wanting anything before.

They only had a few more hours, she reminded herself desperately. There wasn't time. She wasn't ready.

Then Jack smoothed a Band-Aid over the cut and planted a soft kiss in the palm of her hand. When he raised his head, she curled her fingers to hold on to the electric, wildly erotic sensation.

"All better?" he asked, smiling.

"No." Her reply was hardly more than a whisper.

His smile disappeared instantly. "What's the matter?"

"I think… I'm pretty sure…" She swallowed. "No, I know. This is the time."

# *Chapter 10*

Jack stared blankly at the woman perched above him.

"The time for what?"

With a shaky smile, Angela tugged her bandaged hand free of his. To his surprise, she didn't cut small circles or sweeping arcs in the air. Instead, she leaned forward and cupped his face gingerly in her palms.

"You said the next time we kissed it would be for real. You also said that I could pick the time and the place." She brushed her lips across his mouth. "I choose now, Jack. Here."

Astonishment rocked Jack back on his heels. He grabbed for the closest object to steady himself, which just happened to be Angela's thigh. Her *bare* thigh. At the feel of her satiny-smooth skin, astonishment took a back seat to instant need. With an exercise of sheer will, he reined in his sudden, blazing excitement just enough to give her a last out.

"Are you sure, Angela? Here? Now?"

"We'd better take advantage of the opportunities we have," she murmured, tasting the corner of his mouth with the tip of her tongue. "Who knows when disaster will strike again?"

Not in the next few minutes, he prayed, bringing Angela with him as he surged to his feet. Not in the next few hours or days or weeks. Not until he satisfied the craving he'd felt for this woman since the first moment he saw her.

He'd keep it slow, he promised himself as her arms wrapped around his neck and his mouth covered hers. Make it sweet. Take only what she was willing to give.

Too late, he remembered Tony's warning that Angela never did anything by halves. Every promise Jack had just made to himself went up in smoke the moment she molded her body to his. Her breasts pressed against him through the fleece-lined sweatshirt. Her hips tipped into his.

He angled back against the sink, taking her into the cradle of his thighs. She sprawled against his chest, and Jack felt her imprint along the full length of his body. His hands skimmed her waist, her hips, memorizing her shape, fitting her even more intimately against him.

Her tongue met his. Touching. Tasting. Jack slanted his mouth over hers, and knew that touching and tasting wouldn't be enough. He wanted Angela under him, naked. He wanted her mewling with pleasure and moaning in release. He wanted Angela any and every way he could have her.

She pulled back then, breathing hard and fast, and rested her forearms on his chest. Despite his promise to take only what she was willing to give, Jack wasn't sure he could let her go then. To his infinite relief, she didn't try to withdraw.

"Did you—?" She gulped in air. "Did you have your eyes closed?"

"What?"

"It's your turn. To keep your eyes closed."

He shook his head. "We're long past experimenting, sweetheart. This is for real, remember?"

"I remember," she whispered. "Close your eyes, Jack."

Angela's stomach muscles spasmed when his lids slowly lowered. She'd known. Before she leaned over to brush her lips across this man's mouth, she'd known where the kiss might lead. She hadn't wanted to admit it at the time, but Jack had been right when he said that they'd invested something in each other during those moments together on the Fourteenth Street Bridge.

Every touch since then had been leading to this joining of their lips and their bodies. Every moment they were together had been building to this point in time.

Slipping her hands under the cabled fisherman's sweater, she slid her palms up the broad planes of his chest. His heat singed her flesh. His taut muscles jumped under her fingertips. Sheer feminine delight bolted through her. He wanted her. As much as she wanted him. Jack didn't even try to disguise his urgent need. It nudged her in the belly with every ragged breath he took.

Hot, liquid desire spilled into her womb. Angela knew she couldn't stop now if she wanted to, which she didn't. She most certainly didn't.

Her fingers trembling, she drew his sweater up and off. The buttons on his rumpled white shirt resisted her fumbling for only a few seconds. Then her hands smoothed around the soft cotton T-shirt to his back, and the springy hair at the vee neck tickled her lips.

They only had a few hours. Two or three at most, Angela reminded herself. Then the outside world would claim them again. Differing loyalties would tug at them. Danger might stalk them once again. But for now, for these few hours, there was only Jack and her and the sweet, singing need that made her blood rush through her veins and his skin ripple with every touch of her lips and tongue and teeth.

How had she ever imagined him cold? she wondered in those last few moments while her conscious mind still functioned. How had she thought him as inhuman and as calculating as some of the types her family had dealt with in the past few years? He was hot everywhere she touched him, and she touched him everywhere.

Jack stood it for as long as he could, which wasn't long. He'd always been more of a participant than an observer—in his work, in sports. He most definitely wanted to be an equal player when it came to loving this woman. He wanted to touch her as she touched him, everywhere. Taste her as she was tasting him, all over. Breathe in the sight and the scent of her body as it fit itself to his—without the cockeyed seagull as a barrier.

He eased the door open and angled her out of the room before she quite realized his intent. Then he scooped her into his arms and proceeded to scatter the blankets they'd just neatly folded. The lumpy cushions on the shelf/bed/sofa gave under them as Jack followed her down.

His cotton T-shirt got lost in the process. So did the seagull and her sneakers. Her stockinged toes curled into his calves. His palms shaped the swell of her breasts in their covering of black lace. Rock-hard and aching, he positioned her under him.

They were a tangle of straining limbs and slick flesh

and hungry mouths when Jack levered himself up a few inches.

"Wait a minute, sweetheart. Wait."

She groaned. "What for?"

"If we take this any further, we'll need some protection."

Angela heard his low, growled warning over the thunder in her ears. He was giving her a final choice, she realized. Offering one last opportunity to draw back.

It was too late for warnings. Too late to draw back. It had been too late last night, she now knew. The moment Jack donned that ridiculous top hat, her stomach had done a funny little tap dance with her heart, and neither one of them had yet resumed its normal patterns.

"Do you have any protection?" she asked, breathless and embarrassed and shy and meltingly hungry, all at the same time.

He gave her another one of those unrepentant, unabashed grins, the same brand he'd laid on her earlier, when he told her that they'd shared the narrow bed last night.

"I bought some this morning, at the convenience store."

"This morning?" She struggled up on her elbows. "Did you plan on—? I mean, did you think—?"

Jack kept her cradled between his arms. "I hoped. While I held you in my arms last night, I thought about it. A lot."

She fell back, her heart thumping, as he crossed the room and dug in the pocket of his jacket. He came back moments later, shedding the last of his clothes in the process.

Oh, God, he was magnificent. All lean muscle and trim buttocks and long, clean lines. The urgency pounding through her body picked up speed, until it all but consumed her.

Angela didn't know what would come when they left this cabin. At this moment, she didn't care. If she hadn't learned anything else from growing up around the exciting, turbocharged world of the racetrack, she'd learned to give everything she had to this effort, this moment, because she might not get another chance to qualify for the championship circuit. Smiling, she lifted her arms and welcomed him into her heart.

She was so beautiful, Jack thought as he peeled away her remaining layers. So soft and warm, and ticklish in the most surprising places. Like the bend of her elbow, where the skin twitched under his seeking mouth. And the hollowed plane of her belly. And the long, smooth inside curve of her thigh.

Then she took him into her body, and he stopped thinking about anything except pleasuring her as much as she was pleasuring him. Her slick inner heat enveloped him. The friction of their bodies added to the searing heat.

He slid in, and out, and in again. Slowly at first, giving her time to adjust to him, then more rapidly, until he lost himself in her wild rhythm. Angela, Jack rediscovered to his fierce, primal satisfaction, did nothing...*nothing*...by halves.

When he bent to take her stiff nipple in his mouth, she gasped and arched her back to give him easier access. When his need sent him driving into her, she wrapped her legs around his and urged him in an even wilder rhythm. Sliding his hand down her belly, he found her slick, hot core. With thumb and forefinger, he brought her to the edge.

"Jack."

"Now, Angela," he rasped in her ear. "Now, sweetheart. Right here, right now."

She climaxed under him in a spine-arching burst of heat and pure sensation. Then she pulled him with her into the swirling, bright-patterned universe.

They came back to earth slowly. The perspiration that had slicked their bodies cooled. Their breathing gradually slowed. Tugging at one of the blankets, Jack covered them both. Angela pillowed her head on his shoulder, a smug, satisfied smile on her face as she stared up at the ceiling beams.

"Well, well, what do you know? The roof's still intact."

"So it is."

"How long do you think it will stay that way?"

She'd intended the question as a joke, but the moment it was out, her smug smile dimmed by incremental degrees.

With everything that was in him, Jack wanted to promise her that she'd always be safe. That he'd hold her and protect her and shelter her from every storm that might come. He knew enough about Angela Paretti by now, however, to accept that she didn't want sheltering. Holding, though, she didn't seem to mind.

With an easy lift, he rolled her onto his chest. Eyes widening, she balanced herself on her forearms. Her hair fell forward in dark, silky waves.

"Maybe we should try again," Jack suggested, shifting to allow her hips a firmer position against his. "I bet we could blow the roof clear off."

"Again?" she squeaked, her smile slipping back into place. "Don't you have to, um, refuel?"

"That's your job," he told her. "Didn't you tell me that you spent your summers hanging with a pit crew?"

"I'm serious! Do we have time?"

"We've got an hour. Two at most. Think you can manage?"

A wicked glint of laughter entered the brown eyes poised above him. "Do you know how long it takes a NASCAR pit crew to gas, grease, and change all four tires?"

"No."

"Minutes, Jack. Mere minutes."

"Show me."

She showed him. Twice.

When they left the tangle of cushions and blankets some time later, the roof was still firmly attached to the cabin walls.

While Jack finally put the razor and shaving cream he'd purchased earlier to use, Angela slipped on her sweater and tunic. She felt the need to clothe herself in more professional attire for what she knew would be a long, nerve-racking afternoon. She couldn't do much about the whisker burns on her chin, but at least the tunic's high collar disguised the marks on her neck.

She'd just buttoned the last gold button when the phone shrilled. Angela jumped half out of her sneakers, and the bathroom door flew open.

"Don't answer it," Jack instructed tersely, his chest bare and his face lathered with soap.

Another strident ring cut through the sudden stillness.

Angela's heart thumped painfully.

After the second ring, the phone fell silent. The seconds stretched out interminably. When it rang again, Jack visibly relaxed.

"Okay. You can pick it up."

Her pulse slowing from frantic to merely double-time, Angela reached for the receiver. When she heard the voice at the other end of the line, her heartbeat took off again. Swallowing a groan, she greeted her agitated parent. "Hello, Mother."

Across the room, Jack's brows winged. He shouldn't look so surprised, Angela thought wryly. He must have given Tony the telephone code when they were talking at the car, and her brother had probably given it to Maria Paretti in self-defense. It would serve Jack right if Angela made him take the call.

On second thought, she decided, that wouldn't be a particularly wise move. Not after what had just happened. Maria would worm every intimate detail out of him before he knew what hit him. Turning her back on the bare-chested culprit, Angela did her best to soothe her mother's maternal fears.

"No, I can't come home. Not yet.

"I know, I know. But the police are working it.

"Yes, I'm safe."

To her intense relief, Angela discovered that Tony had endorsed her decision to stay at the cabin. She owed him for that. Unfortunately, she soon discovered that her brother had also told Maria Paretti far more about Jack than she needed to know at this confused point. Angela would get him for that.

Her face heating, she mumbled her responses into the phone.

"He's thirty-six.

"Divorced.

"No.

"Maybe."

She rolled her eyes. "I'm sure. Not a drop."

With a low chuckle, Jack retreated to the bathroom.

Angela managed to escape a few moments later. Dropping the receiver onto the phone, she heaved a long, heartfelt sigh, only to half choke on it when the phone shrilled again under her hand.

Jack reappeared on the second ring, wiping his face clean of the remaining lather. Together, they waited through another long pause. When the phone rang again, he answered it. He listened for a few moments, then gave the speaker directions to the cabin.

"Ramirez?" Angela asked.

His gray eyes met hers. "Yes. He's on his way."

This time was over. She knew it. Jack knew it. And neither one of them could say when...or if...the next would come.

Special Agent Manny Ramirez arrived a little over an hour later. As Jack had predicted, he came armed with boxes of financial records, three notebook computers, a fax machine and two harassed-looking accountants.

"You could have picked someplace closer in," he grumbled as they carried a load into the cabin. "We got lost three times trying to find you."

"That was the point," Jack drawled.

Short, wiry, and bristling with nervous energy, the agent dumped his armful of boxes on the kitchen table before raking Angela with a speculative look.

"I'll admit I wasn't too happy when I heard that Merritt read you into this case," he told her frankly. "But I understand you had something to do with the senator's offer of full cooperation this morning."

"The decision to cooperate was his. He doesn't have anything to hide."

"I also understand he wants in on the investigation...assuming we don't implicate him personally, of course."

"You won't."

His black eyes flickered, but he didn't argue. Instead, he rocked back on his heels and relayed a message from Detective Winters.

"Ed said to tell you the lab guys are still doing their thing, and to please call your mother before she calls him again."

Angela stifled a groan. "I talked to her a little while ago."

"Does the lab have any leads yet?" Jack asked, his eyes gleaming at her chagrined expression.

"One. They pieced together enough of the detonator to identify it as part of an arms shipment that was stolen from Fort Benning a few months back. The Bureau's already working with army CID to see if they can find a link to our case."

"You may get help from more than just the army."

The agent frowned. "Oh, yeah? Who else is putting their fingers in our pie?"

"Angela's Uncle Guido is making certain discreet inquiries among his contacts on the street," Jack replied calmly.

She threw him a surprised look. "He is?"

"He is. Tony told me."

"Who's Tony?" Ramirez demanded.

"My brother."

"Your brother?" He made the connection right away. "Your brother is Tony Paretti? No kidding?"

She nodded. "No kidding."

"So who's Guido?"

"My uncle."

"I got that part. Is he a cop?"

"No."

"He's with one of the agencies?"

"Not exactly."

"Then what, exactly?"

"Let's just say he's an independent," Jack interjected. "He and Ed Winters have had some dealings in the past. Ed might not necessarily approve of his methods, but I guarantee you he'll vouch for his reliability in this instance."

Ramirez thrust a hand through his wavy brown hair. "Hell, Jack! Is there anyone else working this case that I should know about?"

"Not that I'm aware of. Why don't you show me what you have here, Manny?"

Shucking his jacket, the agent pulled the lid off one of the boxes and tossed it into a corner.

"I have bank records. I have financial disclosure statements. I have tax returns and telephone logs and trip reports for the past three years. Now you and my friends here have to make sense of them."

Overwhelmed by the sheer volume of data Ramirez had collected, Angela retreated to the sofa/bed while a Jack Merritt she hadn't yet seen emerged. This one was the skilled accountant. The precise, thorough auditor. The consummate number cruncher.

Setting his assistants to work on the financial disclosure forms and tax returns, Jack attacked the bank statements himself. Item by item, record by record, the team scrutinized every financial transaction. Using a spreadsheet Jack set up on the notebook computers, they bounced every bank deposit against reported income from a host of sources. Verified the rates of return on every investment. Tracked every expense, no matter how small, to ascertain whether the senator's outlays exceeded his reported income.

Her stomach hollowing, Angela realized it was just a matter of time until Jack demanded an explanation for the unexplainable.

The moment arrived far sooner than she'd anticipated. Less than two hours after he first delved into the bank records, Jack sat back, frowning.

"This doesn't make sense."

Ramirez jumped up and peered over his shoulder at the computer screen. "What doesn't make sense?"

"The senator's pattern of expenditures for the past year. He's made a number of large cash withdrawals, but I find nothing to show for them. No increase in property insurance to cover significant purchases. No new stocks. No bonds. No real estate transaction or significant charitable contributions."

"How much money are we talking about here?"

"Several hundred thousand."

The special agent whistled. "What do you suppose the senior senator from South Carolina's spending all that money on? Does he have an expensive habit that's gotten out of hand, I wonder? Something our friends at HealthMark might just be willing to help him pay for?"

Jack pulled his gaze from the computer screen. From across the room, he searched Angela's face.

"You won't find a record of those cash expenditures," she confirmed quietly. "The senator gave me that money."

One of the accountants gaped. Ramirez spun around, his eyes bugging.

"Senator Claiborne gave you two hundred thousand dollars?"

"One hundred and ninety-three thousand, seven hundred and fifty-two, to be exact."

"In cash?"

"In cash."

"What for?"

"I can't tell you."

"You can't—?" The agent stuttered in sheer astonishment. "You can't tell me?"

"No."

In the blink of an eye, he went cold and hard and official. His narrowed gaze sliced into Angela.

"Let's get something straight here. I wasn't real happy about your involvement in this case to begin with. If you start obstructing the investigation now, I'm going to become even more unhappy."

"That money has nothing to do with your investigation," she insisted.

"That's not your call."

"That's the one I'm making."

"Look, Ms. Paretti—"

"Hold on, Manny."

His mind racing, Jack rose and crossed to where Angela sat stiff and unmoving on the cushions. A dozen different explanations for the payments occurred to him, some more palatable than others.

The most obvious was that the senator had bailed the Parettis out of their financial hole, but that didn't track with Jack's observation of both Tony and Angela. Neither one would accept out-and-out charity, not to the tune of one hundred and ninety-three thousand dollars.

The idea that the senator had paid Angela for personal services above and beyond her driving duties, Jack dismissed out of hand.

Which left only one remote possibility.

"Does this money have anything to do with the bills Uncle Guido put into circulation?" he asked her, his words low and for her ears only. "Did the senator lend you the money to cover his bad paper?"

"No! He would have, if we'd asked him to, but we managed to catch all but a few of the bills before they hit the street."

"Then what, Angela? What was it for?"

"I can't tell you." Her eyes pleaded with him. "You'll have to trust me on this, Jack. Please."

For one fleeting instant, he recalled the image of the blonde who'd cozied up to him in Tampa. For just that long, his rational, logical mind acknowledged that it was *possible* Angela had chosen this time and this place to capitalize on the undeniable attraction simmering between them. It was *possible* she'd engaged in a desperate attempt to win Jack's trust on her boss's behalf.

As swiftly as that possibility occurred, it collided with a single, absolute certainty. Angela hadn't used her body to entice him. She wouldn't play those kinds of games. Whatever her reasons, she'd given herself wholly, unreservedly. She hadn't been using him then, and he damn well wouldn't use her any longer.

Spinning around, he strode across the room and reached for the phone.

"What are you doing?" Angela demanded, scrambling off the cushioned shelf.

"I'm taking you out of the middle," he told her grimly. "From now on, this is between your boss and me."

# Chapter 11

"What's the senator's private number?" Jack asked, the phone gripped tight in his hand. "I don't want to work my way through a network of underlings."

Angela hesitated, tugged in a dozen different directions. In her heart, she knew Jack was right. He and her boss needed to get face-to-face. Only the senator could explain about the money, and then only to those he absolutely trusted.

Jack needed to understand what drove Henry Claiborne. Needed to glimpse the unshakable core of integrity at the depths of his sometimes devious soul. But the habit of protecting her boss went too deep for her to just hand him over, even to the man she'd welcomed into her arms and her body just hours ago.

"Let me make the call," she said, holding out her hand.

He handed over the phone.

Angela dialed a restricted number on the old-fashioned rotary instrument and waited, her heart pounding. The senator's senior legislative aide answered on the second ring.

"Marc? Is the senator there?"

Marc Green's voice leaped across the wires. "Angela! Where the hell are you? What's going on?"

He sounded as shaken as she'd ever heard him.

"I can't talk right now."

"What do you mean, you can't talk? You have to. I won't operate in the dark like this."

"This doesn't concern you, Marc. Just put the senator on."

She knew instantly that she'd said the wrong thing. For the past few years, she'd tried to keep the confidence and trust Henry Claiborne placed in her from eroding his senior staffer's authority or confidence. She hadn't always succeeded.

Usually, Marc hid his resentment. The only times it surfaced were in the somewhat patronizing explanations he gave visitors of her "special" relationship with the boss, like the one he'd given Jack. And, as now, in an occasional reminder of who was in charge.

"May I remind you that I'm still the senator's legislative director?" he said icily. "Until you take over this position, too, you'd better remember that anything and everything concerning his office also concerns me."

Angela drew in a steadying breath. With Jack and Manny Ramirez and the two accountants listening to the exchange, she had to hold on to her professional cool.

"Marc..." she began placatingly.

The staffer didn't want placating. Ruthlessly he cut her off.

"I want to know what's going on. I want to know

why the boss was late for his meeting with the civic leaders this morning. I want to know why he postponed the hearings on the medical reform bill, and I want to know where the hell you are now.''

Angela didn't lose her temper often, but when she did, she lost it the same way she did everything else. Completely. Wholly. With all the passion of her lively nature.

"Listen to me, Green. I don't have time for your wants right now, and I have even less desire to pander to your conservative, uptight ego. I suggest you put the senator on. Now!''

A frigid silence came over the line.

Angela waited it out. Through the haze of her own anger, she caught Jack's eye. Once again she was reminded of the subtle differences she'd detected between the two men. Although they both worked in the upper echelons of power, Jack wielded his own brand of authority. Marc drew his from his boss.

"The senator's not here," the staffer finally answered coldly. "He left an hour ago.''

"To go where?''

"He wouldn't say.'' The three words might have been chipped from granite. "He left instructions to call his beeper number if we needed him.''

Angela knew instantly where her boss had headed. The same place he went whenever he wanted privacy and peace. As he always did on those occasions when he didn't employ Angela's services, he'd have changed taxis at least once to cover his tracks. Maybe twice, if he'd thought there was a chance that the cabdriver had recognized him.

"Right. I'll talk to you later, Marc.''

"Angela!'' Green made an almost audible effort to

control his temper. "At least tell me if Merritt's with you. Will he be available to testify if we reschedule the hearings for tomorrow?"

"I'll get back to you."

She hung up, knowing she'd have to do some serious ego-soothing with Marc when—if!—she got back to work. The way things were going, that might take a while.

"It sounds as though the senator's legislative director isn't pleased with the fact that he's been left out of the loop," Jack observed.

"His nose is a bit out of joint," Angela conceded, "but he'll get over it."

She hoped.

Dismissing Marc with a wave of one hand, she put herself right back into the middle of Jack's investigation.

"The senator's not at the office. He postponed the hearings and left an hour ago, without saying where he was heading. I think I know where he is. I'll take you there...on one condition."

"No conditions," Ramirez protested. "No deals."

"I'm pretty sure I know where the senator is," she retorted, still fired up from her confrontation with Marc. "You don't. If either of you wants to talk to him any time soon, you agree to my condition."

"Let's hear it."

"I agree."

The two men spoke simultaneously.

Aggrieved, Ramirez turned to Jack. "Wait a minute here. I'm supposed to be the agent in charge of this investigation. You can't just go around making deals without even knowing what the hell they are."

"With Angela I can. I trust her."

Afterward, when she had time to think about it, Angela would pinpoint this moment as the precise instant she suspected she'd fallen, and fallen hard, for the senator's goat. It didn't matter that he was an accountant. That her driving made him nervous. That she didn't know what kind of music he liked or whether he'd support the medical reform legislation or if her mother would approve of him.

He trusted her, and she trusted him, and in Angela's book that formed a bond more binding than the physical one they'd shared such a short time ago.

"Let me make one call," she told the two men, although her smile was for Jack alone. "In private."

"We'll wait outside. Let's go, troops."

"Wait a minute!" Ramirez yelled, grabbing at his coat as he followed his team members outside. "Wait a minute! What's the condition? Is that the condition? A private call? Dammit, Jack!"

Angela made her call, snatched up her purse and joined the others less than two minutes later.

"All right. I'll take Jack and you, Ramirez, to see the senator...if you agree that you won't disclose his location to anyone. *Anyone!* That's the deal. Take it or leave it."

Nodding, Jack pulled open the Chevy's passenger door. "We'll take it."

"Wait a minute!" the agent protested again. "Wait just a damn minute!"

"You wait," Angela said with a grin. "I'm going to burn some rubber."

Ramirez dived into the back seat just as she put the Chevy in gear and hit the gas. A spin of the wheel brought the car around. The rear tires spitting pebbles and oyster shells, the vehicle tore down the narrow lane.

Forty minutes later, Angela pulled into the driveway of a brick house in a rolling suburb that skirted Virginia's famed horse country. Although the sloping front lawn was still winter brown, it had been trimmed and shaped and tended with obvious devotion. A white rail fence surrounded the property, and a matching trellis interwoven with rose stems arched over the brick sidewalk.

Angela bypassed the front door and led the way to a side entrance. While they waited for an answer to the knock, Jack exchanged a look with Manny. From the agent's bemused expression, he couldn't quite place the flamboyant, flashy senior senator from South Carolina in this quiet setting, either.

But it was the senator who answered the door. More or less. Not the white-suited, string-tied suthrun-gentleman image he cultivated so carefully on the Hill. This Henry Claiborne wore a droopy hand-knit sweater, baggy brown pants and well-worn slippers on his stockinged feet.

"Well, well, missy," he boomed, greeting her with a hearty kiss on the cheek. "I know you wanted me to replace the Chrysler, but did you have to blow it up?"

Angela grinned. "Even with the new engine Tony put in, it didn't have enough power to suit me."

A chuckle rumbled deep in his chest. "Nothing will ever have enough power to suit you."

"That's true," she admitted.

Or almost true.

As she stepped into a sunshine-filled kitchen, Angela's mind zinged to a narrow bed. A pair of strong thighs spreading hers. The taut muscles of Jack's back and buttocks as he thrust into her.

He had enough power to suit her. More than enough.

The heady thought sent a spiral of heat through her belly and a rush of warmth into her face. Flustered, she stood back while the senator greeted the two men.

"Well, sir," he told Jack, "I'll admit I thought it would take you a mite longer to untangle my finances, yes, just a mite longer, but I was expecting Angela's call."

"I don't suppose it occurred to you this morning to tell Special Agent Ramirez about the cash withdrawals and save me a few hours' work?" Jack drawled.

One corner of the carroty mustache lifted. "No, as a matter of fact, it didn't."

The short, wiry FDA agent bristled at his genial tone. "This isn't a game, Senator."

"I don't believe I consider it one, either," the legislator replied, his voice deceptively soft. "It was *my* car that blew up last night, and my driver who almost went with it. I don't take kindly to that, sir. Not at all. Someone's going to pay for it, and pay dearly."

Angela hid a smile as Ramirez blinked and took a half step back. Henry Claiborne all bluff and friendly could work his way around the staunchest opponents. The same man soft and sibilant could raise the hairs on a dog's back.

"Let's go into the parlor," he suggested, genial once more, "and we'll have our little chat."

Angela led the way to a sunny front room that held two comfortable armchairs with crocheted doilies pinned to the seat backs and armrests, a nubby plaid sofa and a three-legged sewing basket spilling a colorful array of embroidery threads.

"Hi, Buttons," she cooed, scooping a fat ginger-colored cat off one chair. She tickled it behind the left ear and claimed its seat. Buttons spread like a furry blob across her lap, liberally coating her black tunic and skirt with reddish-brown cat hair, and twitched his left ear patiently until Angela resumed the tickling.

The senator gestured his guests to the sofa and settled himself in the other chair. Steepling his fingers over the paunch disguised by his bulky sweater, he waited for his visitors to fire the opening round.

"We'd like to know about the cash withdrawals you made last year," Jack said evenly. "Withdrawals that amounted to almost two hundred thousand dollars."

"One hundred and ninety-three thousand, seven hundred and fifty dollars, I do believe."

"Fifty-two," Angela put in helpfully.

"Fifty-two," he amended. "Well, son, I gave the money to Angela, as I believe she told you."

"She did. She didn't tell us why, though."

He beamed affectionately at his driver. "She wouldn't. She's too loyal to betray a confidence."

"Too loyal, or too stubborn?" Jack asked with a faint smile.

"Both," she returned. "You'd better remember that, Merritt."

His smile deepened. "I will."

The senator's bushy red brows rose at the exchange. Angela caught the gleam of interest under his heavy lids, and knew she'd have some explaining to do later.

"So what was the money for?" Ramirez asked impatiently, either uninterested in or oblivious of the side currents swirling around him.

"Well, sir, Angela used it to make a down payment on this house. I didn't want the transaction in my name, for reasons of privacy, you understand."

Manny Ramirez was too professional to say a word, but Angela saw his startled gaze dart to her, then to the doilies covering the arms of her chair. When his black eyes came back to her, they were filled with a speculation she'd seen all too many times before. She knew without being told what he was thinking. The same thing so many others thought when they learned that she was more than just the senator's driver.

Ramirez was having trouble envisioning her and the senator in this little love nest, though. Angela couldn't blame him. Neither of them was exactly the doily type.

She wasn't the only one who intercepted the agent's speculative glance. The senator's eyes narrowed, and Jack's glinted a warning. Angela felt a silly rush of happiness at the unmistakable message he telegraphed to the FDA agent. No matter what the evidence, no matter how damning the situation, he wasn't going to accept the obvious.

Special Agent Ramirez was as tough as he looked, however. Not afraid to tackle the issue head-on, he leaned forward and laid it out.

"Let me make sure I understand this. You gave Ms. Paretti one hundred and ninety-three thousand dollars to buy this house."

The senator peered at him óver the peaks of his fingers. "I did."

"You reside here..."

"I reside at my Georgetown town house," Claiborne corrected gently. "Unfortunately, my schedule doesn't allow me to get down here as often as I like."

"You visit here, then, when your schedule—" his face carefully neutral, he nodded toward Angela "—and Ms. Paretti's permit."

"Back off, Manny," Jack instructed, his voice low and even more dangerous than the senator's had been a few moments ago. "You're reading this one wrong."

"I could be. I most definitely could be. But until someone tells me who else lives here besides the senator and—"

"I live here."

The words were so soft, so tentative, that Angela almost missed them. Ramirez, sitting closer to the hall, didn't, however. He slewed sideways on the sofa, his jaw sagging as a silver-haired pixie entered the room.

The senator jumped up. Dismay stripped all the oratory from his voice.

"Lilly! You don't need to get into this."

"I do, Henry," she replied softly.

Angela surged to her feet, almost dumping an indignant Buttons on his head. The cat clawed for purchase in her arms as she rushed across the room.

"It's all right, Lilly. We've got the situation covered."

"I know you do," the delicate-looking woman answered. "You always do. It's all right, Angela. Truly. I heard Henry tell you to bring these gentlemen here only if they promised not to disclose anything about the house to the press."

She turned her aqua eyes to the two men, who'd risen to their feet, as well. "You won't, will you?"

"No, ma'am," Jack answered.

"Hey, wait a minute," Ramirez interjected.

Jack ignored him. "You can trust me."

The tiny woman drifted across the room, trailed by a worried Senator Claiborne and a frowning Angela, with an indignant, ginger-colored fur ball draped over one arm.

"Angela trusted you," the unexpected visitor said. "That's good enough for me."

"It's good enough for me, too, Miss...Ms.?"

"It's Mrs.," the senator said, placing a protective arm around the soft-spoken woman's shoulders. "Mrs. Henry Claiborne."

"I don't believe it," Manny muttered from the back seat of the Chevy a short time later. "They've been married for almost two years, and no one knows about it!"

Gritting her teeth, Angela gave him the same answer she'd already given him three times. "Lilly's a little shy."

"Right," he snorted. "And I'm a little..."

"Dense?" she supplied. "Thick? Suspicious and bureaucratic and narrow-minded?"

"Okay, okay. I get the picture. But two years? And she just visits on weekends and special holidays? Jeez, no wonder Coon Dog Claiborne has such a reputation in this town for playing the field."

Angela shot him an evil glance in the rearview mirror. "Did I say narrow-minded? Let's change that to just plain stupid."

"Shut up, Manny," Jack advised, stomping the floor mat reflexively as the woman beside him took a corner some ten miles per hour faster than he would have. "You're digging yourself into a hole you're never going to get out of."

"What?" The Miami-based agent pulled himself upright after the tight turn. "Are you saying the senator's reputation as a playboy is all a media invention?"

Angela shook her head in disgust. "Of course it is. It's a smoke screen to deflect their attention from Lilly. Which is why I wanted your assurances...your *personal*, one hundred percent, no-kidding assurances..

that none of this business about the house or Lilly leaks out. The media would eat her alive."

"Yeah, well, if we don't find any link between the senator and HealthMark—"

"You won't."

"And if we don't find anything else in his financial records that raises a flag—"

"You won't."

"You have my no-kidding, one hundred percent, personal assurances I won't say anything about Mrs. Claiborne."

"Good."

"But, jeez. Two *years?*"

Jack stretched out his legs and settled in for the ride back to Maryland's western shore. Two years, he mused. His own marriage hadn't even lasted that long.

He'd known before he married Marilyn that their goals were different, but he hadn't realized just how different until it was too late. Sophisticated, well connected and charming, she'd been dazzled by the idea of his grandfather's millions once she found out about them. She'd wanted Jack to reconcile with the man, who had no desire for or interest in reconciliation. She'd engaged her husband in bedroom discussions, dining room debates and, eventually, armed skirmishes over his refusal to join the ranks of Merritt Communications, Inc. She'd finally walked out when he accepted the position at Children's, with its corresponding cut in pay.

Lilly wouldn't walk out on her mate, Jack reflected. Despite her bone-deep shyness, she'd joined her future to the flamboyant, boisterous public figure's.

The senator wouldn't walk out. For two years, he'd protected the woman he loved from the invasive, intrusive aspects of his chosen occupation.

Jack angled his head, studying Angela's face as she sent the Chevy flying along the country roads. She wouldn't walk out. Jack knew that as surely as he knew his own name. She'd give herself passionately. Completely. As she'd given herself to him.

Was it just a few hours ago that they'd shared a narrow bed? Only this morning that they'd twisted and strained in each other's arms? His body stirred at the memory.

How had he come to know and crave this woman more intimately in the short time they'd been together than he had his wife? How could he carry the taste of her mouth and the musky, erotic scent of her more clearly in his senses than any other memory he'd collected in his thirty-six years?

Tony Paretti's words echoed in his mind. *It happens like that sometimes.*

It had happened to Jack on the Fourteenth Street Bridge, when whipped cream and a few moments of violence brought Angela into his arms for the first time.

Now he had to find a way keep her there.

Safely.

Slathered in whipped cream wouldn't be bad, either, he decided with a tight smile.

He was still enjoying that image when Angela spun the wheel and took a sharp turn into a shopping center full of trendy boutiques and gourmet coffee shops. Both Jack and Manny jerked into instant alertness.

"Why the detour?"

"Is someone following us?"

Angela pulled the Chevy to her customary screeching halt and cut the engine.

"No one's following us," she announced into the

taut silence. "But I refuse to spend another hour in these clothes. Hang tight."

Manny's jaw dropped as she slammed the car door and headed for a shop displaying mannequins draped in a dazzling display of jewel-toned wools.

"What the hell is this?"

"I think she's going shopping," Jack drawled.

"She's going shopping? I'm up to my ass in one of the biggest investigations of my career, and she's going shopping?"

Jack shouldered open the passenger side door. "I've got to pick up a few things, too."

Like clean underwear.

And a fresh shirt.

And whipping cream.

## *Chapter 12*

Four hours later, Jack tilted back in his chair and admitted what Angela had staunchly maintained all along. There wasn't any link between Senator Claiborne and HealthMark. Not one that Jack and his two weary assistants could find, anyway.

"We've still got to check a few transactions that went through offshore banks," he told Manny. "But we're talking small bucks. A repayment of a loan made to a friend in one instance. A campaign contribution from a Jamaican sugarcane grower in another."

The FDA agent nudged aside the remains of the carryout fried-fish dinner he'd procured earlier from the village and planted his elbows on the table. "So you think he's clean?"

As clean as any man who'd spent forty years in politics, Jack thought cynically. Henry Claiborne had accepted huge honoraria for speaking engagements before the current ceilings went into effect a few years ago.

He'd hobnobbed with kings and princes, who'd show-ered a small museum's worth of gifts on him. A good number of these gifts had been reported. A good many more, Jack suspected, had not. The senator also just happened to own a large chunk of property in a wood-land area that one of his fellow legislators had recom-mended for purchase by the U.S. Park Service.

None of these issues related to the one that had brought Jack to Washington, however.

"He's clean, as far as HealthMark is concerned," he replied, linking his hands behind his head.

A pointed what-did-I-tell-you "Ahem" drifted from the other side of the cabin. Over the top of his notebook computer, Jack eyed the woman curled up in the over-stuffed chair. To her credit, Angela didn't do more than smirk back at him.

Even with a smirk on her face, though, Jack had to admit she looked incredible. The cowl-necked sweater in a rich ruby red that she'd picked up during her shop-ping spree brought out the luster of her dark eyes and hair. And the stonewashed jeans that clung to her slen-der lines and supple curves had made it difficult for Jack to concentrate these past four hours. Those high-topped sneakers hadn't helped, either. The red hearts had flashed distractedly with every idle swing of her foot.

"What happens now?" she asked, abandoning the armchair to join the small group clustered around the table.

Ramirez reached for a cardboard box. "We'll take this stuff back to headquarters with us and check those offshore transactions when the banks open tomorrow."

Shaking her head, Angela handed him a stack of computer printouts. "You're wasting your time."

"Yeah, well, maybe."

It was as close as Manny would get to an affirmative. As Jack had discovered in the months he'd worked with him, the investigator had the tenacity of a pit bull. He didn't give up on a lead until it was stone-cold dead.

Nor did he want to give up on this case. As Manny didn't hesitate to admit, the HealthMark investigation was one of the biggest he'd ever been involved in, with the potential for stiff criminal sentences and millions of dollars in fines. He wanted every charge nailed down, every scrap of evidence documented.

So did Jack. Or he had, until a midnight-blue Chrysler went up in flames, almost taking Angela with it. His priorities had now shifted. He didn't want anything or anyone involved in this case stone-cold dead.

"You're wasting your time here," Angela repeated stubbornly, jamming another stack of records into the half-filled box. "You won't find anything in those off-shore whatevers. And if you don't find anything, where does that leave us?"

"Back where we were when your car blew up," Ramirez admitted grudgingly. "With a whole bunch of questions and no answers."

Not quite where they were last night, Jack thought. He was now convinced that the senator's summons to Washington was related to his proposed medical reform legislation, and only to the legislation. Which left only two possible explanations for the car bomb and, Jack suspected, the shooting.

Someone wanted to prevent him testifying.

Or wanted to silence Angela.

The former proposition he could handle. The latter created a hard, cold lump of determination in the pit of his stomach.

He waited until Angela had carried a box out to the

assistants busily engaged in loading the van before he cornered Manny.

"I want you to talk to your contacts at Justice tonight," he instructed. "Tell them it's time to move on this case. We've given them enough, more than enough, to issue indictments."

"They're not ready to move," the agent protested. "They think they can catch a few more fish in this net. So do I, for that matter."

"We've caught enough. Let's start reeling them in."

"I'm not sure Justice will agree."

Jack's jaw hardened. "I'm not giving them a choice. Tell them they've got until tomorrow afternoon to get their stuff together, then I'm going public."

Manny thumped down the box he'd been holding. "Tomorrow afternoon!"

"The senator kept his end of the bargain. I'm keeping mine. I'm going to testify before his subcommittee."

The agent's shrewd gaze darted to the partially open front door. Angela's figure was an indistinct blur in the deep purple twilight.

Jack knew Manny hadn't been blind to the interplay between Angela and him this afternoon. Nor did it take the FDA agent long to connect her involvement in the investigation with Jack's sudden desire to rip away the shroud of secrecy.

"Look," Manny said doggedly, "if this is about the shooting and the car bomb, we still don't know that either of those incidents were connected to our case. Give us a little more time. Let us track down all the leads."

Jack shook his head. "I've been willing to walk point for you up to now, but I'm not willing to let anyone else get caught out there with me."

"Anyone else? Or anyone Angela?"

"Just tell your contacts at Justice to get those indictments written out and the marshals ready to knock on a few doors tomorrow."

Ramirez drummed his fingers on the tabletop. Head cocked, he studied Jack thoughtfully.

"You're setting yourself up, aren't you?"

"Maybe."

"You're going to stroll up the steps of the Capitol Building tomorrow, as bold as brass. If someone's trying to stop you from testifying, that will be their last chance, because after that, the case will break wide open."

"That's the way I see it."

"Why, Jack? Why not just let us keep you and Angela nice and safe and out of sight until we discover which of you was the target?"

"What if you never pin that down? What if the trail is so well covered, you never find out who or why?"

"Yeah, well, there's always that possibility."

"I'm done working with probabilities and possibilities. If I'm the one they're after, I want to force their hand. Tomorrow."

"And if you're not?"

Jack's eyes narrowed. "Then we throw every resource at our disposal in with Ed Winters and the Parettis to find out who's after Angela."

It didn't take Angela much longer than it had Manny to grasp the implications of Jack's decision to testify. As the tan-colored van's taillights disappeared, he suggested she call the senator and his senior staffer to confirm the hearing on the following day.

Her head swung around. "You're going to testify? In support of the senator's proposed legislation?"

"Yes, to the first. Not necessarily, to the second." His hand shot up to forestall her protest. "I'll share my views and answer any questions I'm asked, but I'm still not convinced that increased government regulation is the answer to the problems in our health care system."

"You'll answer any questions?" she repeated. "Even about HealthMark and Gromorphin?"

"Yes."

Her foot tapped the pine floor as she digested that one. After a moment, deep parallel grooves appeared between her brows.

"You're calling their hand, aren't you?"

"I'm going to try."

The grooves disappeared, and a determined glint came into her brown eyes. "Good! We'll smoke the bastards out, Jack. Then we'll burn them."

Her fierce avowal didn't surprise him. Jack had suspected that Angela wouldn't protest his decision. But he still wasn't prepared for the way she threw herself so completely and intently into the fray.

"I'll call the senator," she said, heading for the phone. "Then Marc Green. If he sets the hearing up for late afternoon, that will allow time for word to get out to all interested parties. We can—"

He caught her arm. "Before you call anyone, I want you to understand one thing. There's no 'we' involved. Not tomorrow."

"What are you talking about?"

"I don't want to expose you to any more danger than I already have. Manny's going to arrange a driver and set up the route in."

He expected fireworks. He anticipated a storm of protest and hands slashing through the air. Instead, she folded her arms over the front of her sweater and locked her eyes with his.

"Let's get something straight, Merritt. I've been trained in offensive and defensive road techniques, escape and evasion and counterterrorist measures. All that aside, no one—I repeat, no one—can overtake a Paretti in the lead position."

"Is that right?"

"That's right."

She looked so fierce, so determined, that Jack almost conceded. But his need to protect her went far too deep at this point. The seeds of that need had been sown on the Fourteenth Street Bridge. They'd germinated while he watched her handle the Browser. When the Chrysler lifted off the ground, they'd wrapped their roots tight around his heart.

Angela soon disabused him of the notion that he had the final say in the matter, however. Hands on hips, she laid it on the line.

"I'm your driver. Period. Until this is over, at least. Then I think we need to talk about future roles and missions."

She was right. Jack knew she was right. Whatever would come between them had to wait until this was over. But he couldn't have stopped himself from taking her in his arms at that moment any more than he could have stopped breathing.

"We'll do more than talk," he promised, imprinting every sculptured curve and shaded hollow of her face in his memory.

Angela ran the tip of her tongue over suddenly dry lips. The shimmering, tingling sensation that overtook her whenever she got too close to this man worked its way in from her fingertips and up from her toes, until her entire body shivered. Her heart hammering, she shaped his chin and cheeks with her palms.

"I'm going to make my calls to the senator and to Marc," she said. "Then you call Manny and Ed Winters and tell them when we'll be coming in tomorrow. *We,* Jack. You and me. Together."

His arms tightened around her. "And after the calls?"

She brushed his lips with hers. "After the calls, we review the draft of the senator's legislation. It's still in my purse."

"You're kidding, right?"

"Nope. I'm not giving up on you yet, Merritt. Of course," she murmured against his mouth, "the night's still young. We might just take another shot at besting the all-time NASCAR record for refueling."

When he brought her up hard against his body, Angela seriously considered changing the sequence of events. Despite her teasing about beating the record, she had no intention of rushing things. Not tonight. Maybe not ever.

Jack must have had the same idea.

"Make your calls," he growled. "I'll make mine. Then you've got one hour, I repeat, one hour, to talk. About anything."

The senator, of course, grasped the implications of Jack's decision to testify immediately.

"So he's thinking to use my hearings to bait a trap, is he? Well, this ol' coon hunter might just be able to help him tree a varmint or two. I'll spread the word that this is going to be a humdinger of a session." His voice sharpened. "You just be careful, missy, you hear?"

"I will."

"And make sure that man of yours keeps his head down and his seat belt buckled."

"He's not mine," she protested with a quick glance over one shoulder. "Not yet, anyway."

"Ha! My eyesight may be failing me a bit these days, but it's still good enough to catch those looks you were giving our friend Jack this afternoon. Do you know what they say back home 'bout folks who go around kissin' goats, by the way?"

"No," she replied hastily, "and I don't want to."

He chuckled again, then hung up after issuing a stern admonition for her to call her mother.

She called Marc Green instead.

Marc's reaction to the confirmation of Jack's appearance before the committee was far more restrained than his boss's. A frigid silence spun out over the line, causing Angela to bite back an impatient sigh. The staffer was still obviously in a snit over their earlier confrontation.

Too bad! She didn't have either the time or the inclination to soothe his ruffled ego. After confirming the time of the hearing, Angela hung up. Then she dug her dog-eared copy of Senate Bill 693 out of her purse and plopped down next to Jack on the narrow cushions.

"One hour," he warned, marking the time with a pointed look at his watch. "Assuming I can keep my mind on medical reform and my hands off you for that long."

"One hour," she agreed, hoping she could keep her mind on medical reform and her hands off *him* for that long.

Despite their banter and the heavy sense of anticipation that gripped them both, the gravity of the issues they grappled with soon consumed them. Angela didn't convince Jack to support all the provisions of the bill. In truth, she didn't understand a good many of them. Those areas she had personal knowledge of, however, she campaigned for skillfully and enthusiastically. Jack didn't argue, nor did he dispute the issues involved. He simply fed them back to her from a different perspective.

True, some of the most expensive drugs on the market only cost a few dollars, at most, to mass-produce. Pharmaceutical companies had to recoup their overhead and operating costs, however, as well as the ten to twenty years of research that went into developing, testing and obtaining FDA approval to market those drugs. Government-imposed price controls would certainly cut costs to the consumer in the short term. In the long term, those same controls could discourage vital research that might save lives.

Yes, all citizens should have equal access to the health care system, regardless of income levels. But patients' needs and desires weren't equal. In a federally regulated system, should taxpayers be asked to fund elective cosmetic surgery? Or prolonged life support for patients whose loved ones couldn't bear to let them go? Any system of guaranteed care still had to allow for individual options and needs, Jack suggested.

Page by page, subparagraph by subparagraph, he pointed out the strengths and weaknesses in the proposed legislation to an attentive and secretly impressed Angela. She'd listened to endless debates in the senator's office, when lobbyists for the AMA and the major insurance companies protested vehemently against every provision and suggested alternatives. None of the arguments she'd heard made the sense Jack's did.

He tapped a finger on a small paragraph at the bottom of the next-to-the-last page. "This insert, for example, is pure dynamite."

Frowning, she peered at the article in question. "I don't remember that insert in the original version of the bill. But what's wrong with tax incentives for clinics and nursing homes that provide quality care to their patients at a reduced cost?"

"On the surface, nothing. But a growing number of nursing homes and special-care clinics are multinational corporations with other interests in the health industry. HealthMark, for example, operates a drug distribution unit, a home infusion unit, and oncology clinics all across the country. This language would grant them tax credits for providing their own drugs to the cancer clinics at a slight discount…which they already do."

"I'm sure that wasn't the intent," Angela admitted, hooking her arms around her drawn-up knees. "Marc will have to change the wording before the bill goes to full committee."

"Yes, he will."

The dog-eared and heavily underlined papers fluttered as Jack scanned the last page, then fanned through the bound copy of the bill a final time.

"There are some good provisions here, Angela," he said slowly. "And a great many more I adamantly oppose. If I'm asked my opinion, I'm going to give it."

She pressed her lips together, pulled by divided loyalties. Coon Dog Claiborne was an expert at extracting precisely the testimony he wanted from the most reluctant witnesses. She knew his strategy. She'd seen him in action countless times.

In this instance, he intended to keep his questions to Jack focused exclusively on the audits of HealthMark and the abuses they'd uncovered. Then he'd hold those abuses up as proof of the need for sweeping reform. That was why he'd brought Jack to Washington.

"You may not be asked for an opinion," she told him, bending her allegiance as far as it would go. "You don't know the senator. He, ah, scripts his agenda very carefully."

"He doesn't know me, either." His gaze settled on her face. "Neither do you, for that matter."

It was true. Aside from the bare facts in the brief bio the staff had pulled together, Angela knew little about his private life. Strangely, she didn't care.

"I know all I need to know, Jack," she told him softly.

The quiet words hung on the air between them. He tucked a loose strand of hair behind her ear and cupped her cheek.

"What do you know, Angela?"

She rested her cheek in his palm, loving the feel of its warmth against her skin. She was close, very close, to loving the man that went with it.

"I know you're willing to try food you can't even pronounce."

"That's important?"

"It is to me."

His thumb stroked her chin. "What else?"

"I know you look pretty darn good in a top hat."

The slow stroking moved to her lower lip. "You think so, huh?"

She planted a kiss on the pad of his thumb. "I do."

"What else?"

Her mouth curved. "I know that you've got a way to go until you break the NASCAR refueling record."

Laughter leaped into his eyes. "Guess I need more

practice. With someone who can find her way around
the pits.''

"Well...I've got a few hours with nothing to do. I
suppose I could let you practice on me.''

The phone's shrill cry dragged them from a sound
sleep. Jack rolled off the narrow bed, and was on his
feet before the sound had fully penetrated Angela's consciousness.

Groggy and disoriented, she pushed herself up on one
elbow. "Wh—?''

The single overhead bulb flared into light on the second ring, illuminating the hard planes and shadowed
valleys of Jack's body. Every tendon corded with tension, he poised over the phone.

Silence descended. Five seconds. Ten.

Angela tried desperately to adjust to the sudden sense
of danger that invaded her sleep-clogged brain. She'd
forgotten. Lost in Jack's arms, she'd forgotten that there
was another world outside this cabin. She almost sobbed
in relief when the phone shrilled again.

Jack picked it up immediately. "Yes?''

His gaze snagged hers from across the room. For the
life of her, Angela couldn't decipher the sudden glint
in his eyes.

"Yes, Mrs. Paretti, she is.''

Oh, God! Her Mother! And Jack. Naked.

Well, one of them was naked, anyway. Her mother
was probably encased from neck to knee in the hot-pink
nightie Tony had bought her last Mother's Day.

"No, ma'am,'' Jack said, holding her eyes. "Not a
drop.''

Groaning, Angela flopped back on the cushions and

threw her arm over her face. She kept it firmly in place until the call ended, some moments later.

"Please," she begged. "Tell me I'm having a bad dream. Tell me my mother didn't just ask you if you had any Italian blood."

"Your mother didn't just ask me if I had any Italian blood. Your aunt Rose did."

Angela dropped her arm. "Aunt Rose? Uncle Guido's wife?"

Mustachioed, gimlet-eyed and iron-willed, the formidable Rose Paretti ruled her household with the efficiency and ruthlessness of a dictator. She was one of the reasons her poor uncle retreated to this comfortable, cluttered crab shanty as often as possible.

Angela scrambled to sit up, dragging the covers with her. "Why in the world did Aunt Rose call?"

"She's relayed a message from your uncle Guido. I'm supposed to get in touch with Ed Winters right away. Hang on."

Her mind whirling, Angela listened to Jack's side of the conversation with Ed Winters, which seemed to consist primarily of *I'll be damned*s. He hung up a few moments later and stared at the cabin wall.

"Well?" she demanded. "What's going on?"

He gave himself a little shake, the way a dog might as it came awake.

"I caught Ed just as he was heading downtown. It seems that someone deposited a garbage can on the front steps of the Second District headquarters a little while ago. Two patrolmen found it...and the man who'd been stuffed in headfirst."

Angela clutched the blankets to her chest. She now knew where this was heading. Uncle Guido's connections had delivered.

A skilled printer and bookbinder when he received his long-awaited visa to the States in the late thirties, Guido Paretti had forged papers for several friends who weren't as fortunate. Those friends had never forgotten the favor. One was now the mayor of a large Eastern Seaboard city. He'd invited Guido to his swearing-in. Another had recently sold his string of Las Vegas hotels for an undisclosed sum. The garbage can, Angela had been told, was his personal signature.

"Ed Winters says this human trash might be our hired hit man."

She surged up on her knees, her heart thumping wildly. "Really?"

"According to the patrolmen," Jack said slowly, "the guy fits your description, although he's closer to thirty than twenty."

She dismissed the extra decade with a wave of one hand. "I only saw him for a second or two."

"He's also scared out of his gourd," Jack continued, "and spilling his guts. He keeps babbling that he has no idea who hired him, that all the arrangements were made via anonymous calls. But he swears on his mother's grave that he didn't know a relative of Guido the Ragman would be with the suit he was supposed to take out."

"Oh, Jack!"

She was across the room and in his arms in seconds, blankets and all. She clung to him, her stomach roiling.

In her heart of hearts, she'd suspected all along that Jack was the target of these horrible attacks. But knowing made it worse.

So much worse.

Jack wrapped his arms around her and buried his face in her tumbled hair. He'd suspected—hoped!—all along that he, and not Angela, was the target. Knowing made what he had to do easier.

So much easier.

## Chapter 13

As she always did, Angela tried hard not to wake up.

Dragging the blankets over her head to shut off the sunlight streaming through the cracks in the curtains, she burrowed her face into the cushions. Their musty odor was almost gone, she noted in a lazy corner of her mind. Now, Jack's scent lingered on the layers covering the cushions, a healthy male residue of warmth and exertion. Of love and lust.

A languid heat swirled through her as she reveled in both the scent and the memories of the night just past. They'd come close, she mused dreamily. They'd come darn close to besting the NASCAR record for refueling. Once after Jack had tossed the senator's bill aside, and once after Aunt Rose's call, when they'd...

The delicious heat evaporated instantly.

Aunt Rose's call!

The garbageman!

Jack!

Yanking at the tangle of blankets, Angela poked her head out and searched the tiny cabin. She went limp with relief when she spotted Jack at the kitchen table, clicking away on the little notebook computer Manny Ramirez had left for his use.

He'd obviously been up for some time. His hair was sleek and wet and slicked back in the way that reminded her so much of the Fonz. He'd pulled on the warm, bulky-knit fisherman's sweater, and he wore the brown cord slacks he'd purchased yesterday. Judging by his attire, he wasn't going anywhere. Not for a while.

He was safe and here and hers for a few hours more.

Wiggling out of the confining blankets, Angela pushed herself up and indulged in a long, catlike stretch. Her head fell back, and the soft cotton of the T-shirt Jack had insisted she pull on for warmth last night molded to her skin.

Her movement drew Jack's intent gaze from the flickering computer screen. Instant, aching arousal gripped him at the sight of Angela arching to greet the morning. With her hair spilling down her back and the tips of her breasts peaking in the cool morning air, she looked so much like the pagan goddess he'd first imagined her that it was all he could do not to cross the room, tumble her back onto the bed and lose himself in her wild, welcoming warmth.

As intense as that urge was, however, he wouldn't allow it to override the task he'd set himself, the task that had pulled him out of her arms just before dawn. He contented himself with enjoying the sight of Angela's long, slender legs as she swung off the bed and padded across the room, wearing only his T-shirt and a sleepy smile.

"What are you doing?"

"Crunching some numbers."

Her nose wrinkled. "I can think of better ways to start the day."

Smiling, Jack leaned back in his chair and linked his hands behind his head. "Like how?"

She leaned a hip against the edge of the table. "Well, we could go for a walk along the shore. Or we could drive into the village and stuff ourselves silly with grits and crab cakes. Or—" she waggled her eyebrows "—we could try one more time to beat the record."

Although she kept the banter light and easy, Angela was serious. Absolutely, one hundred percent, no-kidding serious. The knowledge that Jack would soon leave the safety of this small pine-shingled cabin and set himself up as a target ate at her insides like battery acid. For all her passionate insistence that she, and she alone, would drive him to the Capitol, she had the cowardly urge to hide the car keys, disable the starter and curl up with him for the next week or month or year.

"I vote for all of the above," he responded with a lazy smile. "But I want to show you something first."

"What?"

"These numbers I've been working on."

"All right," she said doubtfully. "But I think you should know I'm a lot better at things mechanical than things mathematical."

She leaned over to peer at the gray computer screen. In the process, the T-shirt pulled up one hip. Jack's smile got a little tight around the edges.

"These figures may take a while to explain," he told her. "Why don't you pull on something warmer...and less distracting?"

For all of two seconds, Angela was tempted. Very tempted! If a mere glimpse of her bare hip could distract the bean counter in Jack from all those neat columns of figures, she had a good idea what might happen if she scooted his little notebook computer to one side, perched on the table and curled her toes in his lap.

As quickly as the idea darted into her mind, Angela discarded it. Despite their lighthearted banter, reality was fast closing in. Whatever Jack wanted to show her had something to do with the reason they were secluded away together in the first place. This wasn't the time to play games. Unfortunately.

With a wave of a hand, she headed for the bathroom. "I'll get cleaned up and dressed. Just sit tight."

He wasn't going anywhere, Jack thought, slewing his attention back to the computer screen. Not until he made sense of the numbers. Leaning forward, he hit the keyboard again.

He was still playing with the spreadsheet he'd developed when Angela reappeared, scrubbed, brushed and fully clothed. She'd tied her hair back in a loose ponytail and pulled on her figure-hugging jeans and the warm, fleecy sweatshirt with the cockeyed seagull on the front. Hauling the other chair around to Jack's side of the table, she plopped down in it and peered at the computer screen with the same enthusiasm she might give a dentist's drill.

"What do we have here?"

"Do you remember that language in the senator's bill? The one that grants tax incentives to clinics and nursing homes to reduce costs to their patients?"

"Yes."

"I woke up this morning thinking about it."

That certainly put a dent in her ego, Angela thought. Jack had awakened with his mind on tax incentives. She had zinged right to lust and love and a fervent wish that she could stay burrowed under the covers with him for the rest of the day.

"I decided to test the language in the clause with some actual numbers," Jack continued.

She hunched forward and peered at the rows and columns on the screen. "Where did you get the numbers?"

"The computer has a built-in modem. I just dialed up EDGAR."

"Edgar Who?"

"The FTC's Electronic Data Gathering and Retrieval System."

"No kidding? You broke into the Federal Trade Commission's files?"

"It's on the Internet. You just have to know how to get to it."

"Right."

"Using that information, I constructed a chart showing the reported revenue for six highly diversified, well-established companies."

He hit the tab key several times. The cursor moved across the spreadsheet on the screen, highlighting a series of numbers as it marched from left to right.

"Then I did a pro forma analysis to calculate what their revenue would have been if the tax incentives in this bill had been in place last year."

Angela shook her head helplessly. "You've already lost me."

"Sorry. Here, look." He moved the cursor to a cell at the bottom of the spreadsheet. "This is HealthMark's reported revenue from all sources."

Angela gulped at the staggering number of zeros in the highlighted number.

"Got that?" Jack asked.

"Yes."

"Now I'll show you what their income would have been had the tax incentives proposed in this bill been in effect last year."

He put the cursor on a long, complex formula in the entry bar and changed a couple of numbers. Angela gaped as the sum in the total-revenue cell jumped from staggering to mind-boggling.

"Good grief!"

"My sentiments exactly."

"But...but..."

She struggled to understand how anyone could have let a provision like this slip through. With all the lawyers on the Hill, surely one of them should have caught it. Jack put his own interpretation on its inclusion.

"The language in this provision isn't loose or careless. It guarantees a specific benefit to a limited number of companies, HealthMark among them. Whoever inserted this paragraph knew exactly what he was doing. I'm guessing he was paid for it, too. Handsomely."

Angela swung around on her chair. "I thought we settled the question of whether or not HealthMark bought off the senator!"

"It's settled in my mind. The question I want answered now is who else could have slipped this language into the bill."

His even reply took the heat from Angela's instant, ready defense of her boss. She dredged her memory, trying to remember who or when or how that small paragraph had come into being.

"I don't think that wording was in the original draft. The bill's gone through so many revisions, though, I'm not sure."

"Can we do an audit trail? Track the revisions and find out who authored that particular paragraph?"

"Sure. Marc Green keeps a history file of every piece of legislation, and a working file of all bills the senator sponsors. In fact, he's the one who—"

Her breath caught.

"The one who what?"

"Who has to incorporate the changes that are hammered out in committee or in conference into the final draft," she finished, her heart thumping painfully.

A cool gray filter seemed to settle over Jack's eyes. "Tell me about Marc Green. Manny ran a routine check on him before I came up here, but we didn't find anything to snag our interest."

Angela jumped up and began to pace. "Of course you wouldn't find anything! Marc is a...a..."

"A what?"

She flung out her hands. "He's a staffer! The ultimate staffer! He doesn't have a life other than the Hill, not one that any of the rest of us know about, anyway. He's in the office when we come in, and there long after we all go home. He's only taken one vacation in all the time I've worked for the senator."

Jack's expression remained shuttered behind the steel of his eyes.

"Marc's at the pinnacle of power," Angela argued. "Or as close to it as he can come without being elected to office. He wouldn't risk his career or his position by...by playing into HealthMark's hands."

"Reflected power can corrupt as easily as the real thing."

Jack was right, of course. Angela was a student of politics, as well as a firsthand observer. She knew how easily power could and did corrupt. But Marc...?

She wasn't sure why she was defending him so vigorously. She didn't really like him, any more than he liked her. They'd worked together for almost three years, though, and she couldn't bring herself to believe he would betray their boss or...or try to harm her.

Shivers raced down her arms. Once again, she heard the blast that had split the night. Once more, she saw the Chrysler engulfed in flames.

As it had the night of the bombing, Jack's voice penetrated the swirling vortex of her thoughts. Steady. Calm. Precise.

"Let's take this one step at a time. When we met in his office, Green said that he'd tried to discourage the senator from inviting me to testify. Why?"

Angela wrapped both arms around her middle and drew in a deep breath. Forcing herself to put aside her instinctive defense of a man she'd always respected, if not always liked, she thought back to the days before Jack's summons to Washington.

"Marc cited the same reasons you gave the senator for not wanting to appear before the committee. Your data was too raw. The implications were too far-reaching to disclose without extensive analysis. And, as Marc pointed out, we didn't know what you might say. We still don't," she added pointedly.

Jack ignored her aside. "All right. If we assume Green had other, more personal reasons for not wanting me to testify, we can assume he had something to do with that incident on the bridge. He knew what flight I was coming in on."

Her stomach lurched. "He also knew the exact moment we left National Airport. I called in to the office, remember?"

"I remember," he said grimly. "I also remember that

Green was present when the senator sent us off to dinner in his personal vehicle. It wouldn't have taken much effort to track the Chrysler to your cousin's lot.''

She dropped back into the chair, feeling sick.

Jack yanked up the phone receiver. ''I'm going to get hold of Manny.''

It took some minutes to track the special agent down at the Justice Department, where, he informed Jack in a huff, he was up to his ass in indictments.

''Let the lawyers work the paper, Manny. I want you to pull out all the stops and find out everything you can on the senator's legislative director. Yeah, that's right. Marc Green.''

As she listened to the exchange, Angela felt the first stirring of wrath. Bit by bit, her anger edged out the sick feeling in her stomach. By the time Jack had finished with Manny and put in another, shorter call to Ed Winters, she'd worked up a healthy head of steam.

''That bastard!'' she hissed. ''That...suspender-wearing bastard!''

''We don't know for sure he's behind any of this,'' Jack reminded her.

''No, we don't. But I'll tell you this. If he is, he's going to be one sorry staffer.''

She jumped up and marched across the room. Snatching up the faithful football jacket, she shoved her arms into the sleeves and jabbed at the front snaps.

''Let's go get something to eat. Then, Dr. Merritt, I'm going to call my mother.''

''Your mother?''

''Right. My mother.'' Eyes glinting with determination, she headed for the front door. ''You're not the only one who can bait a trap.''

* * *

By ten o'clock that morning, she was ready to set the bait. Swiping her damp palms down the sides of her black skirt, Angela reached for the phone. Jack's hand closed over hers, pinning it to the receiver.

"You don't have to do this."

"Yes, I do."

"I'll call him, Angela."

Her mouth set. "No. It should come from me."

Slowly, Jack lifted his hand. He didn't like this. He'd told her so repeatedly during breakfast and after. But Manny Ramirez's excited call a few minutes ago had convinced him.

The special agent had confirmed what Angela had told Jack earlier. Marc Green had taken only one vacation in years, a two-week cruise to the Galapagos Islands. Since this constituted such a departure from his established routine, they'd contacted the cruise line and discovered that Green had shared a cabin with a woman by the name of Katherine Palmer.

Ms. Palmer, Manny reported gleefully, was a striking thirty-four-year-old redhead...who just happened to work for HealthMark, Incorporated, as a midlevel PR executive.

The bastard, Angela thought again. Lifting the receiver, she dialed Marc's private number at the office.

He answered on the first ring.

"Marc? This is Angela."

Her eyes locked with Jack's.

"Yes, he's still planning to testify. But he wants to talk to the senator first. If the traffic's not too bad on I-95 south once we hit the Beltway, I'll get him there by two."

Her fingers tightened.

"No, I'm driving Tony's Corvette. You know how fast that baby can move. Right."

Angela replaced the receiver and stood staring at it for long, silent seconds.

"I wonder how long it will take before the garbage-man gets another anonymous call?" she asked softly.

It didn't take long.

Less than fifteen minutes later, Ed Winters reported that their quarry had taken the bait.

The sweating hit man, still shaken from his recent encounter with the trash can and surrounded by a team of agents and detectives, had received a call traced to a pay phone in St. Augustine, Florida. Angela wasn't surprised at the location. Jack had warned her that Marc would undoubtedly use a middleman for his arrangements. Still, Ed Winters's terse report left her shaken.

This time, he told her and Jack, the hit man's task was to take out the passenger in a restored red '68 Corvette that would be traveling south on I-95 into the District sometime before two o'clock this afternoon.

His eyes hard and cold, Jack tossed her the football jacket. "Come on. We're going for that walk we talked about earlier."

"Now?"

"Now! We've still got a couple hours. We're going to let the cold air clear our heads...and I'm going to do my damnedest to convince you to stay here this afternoon."

"You're wasting your breath, Merritt."

He tried. She had to give him that. He certainly tried. Jack could be darned convincing when he wanted to, she discovered. But he wasn't anywhere near as convincing as she was stubborn. The wind off the Chesapeake whipped her hair around her face as she matched him stride for stride and argument for argument.

"You're not going in alone," she insisted after a long, heated debate. "Not unless you knock me unconscious, or leave me here bound and gagged."

"I'm considering both options," he replied, his jaw tight.

Shocked, she stopped in her tracks. "You wouldn't!"

When he turned to face her, Angela saw that he would. Incensed, she planted both fists on her hips.

"Now, you listen to me, Jack Merritt. We're in this together. We have been since the first shot was fired across the bridge."

"That doesn't mean we have to be together when the last shot is fired. I don't want you hurt, Angela."

"I don't want *either* of us hurt. That's why we're going to leave this cabin at precisely one o'clock. Together. We're going to drive into the city. Together. We're going to confront Marc Green. Together. Then you're going to testify before the senator's subcommittee, after which we're driving to Baltimore. Together."

The hard line of his jaw eased. "Baltimore, huh?"

"Baltimore."

She threw back her head, her eyes snapping with promise of things to come.

"I'm not facing my mother alone. You're going with me, even if I have to knock you unconscious and throw you in the back seat, bound and gagged."

"You think you could?"

"I know it." She rocked back on her heels. "I told you that Tony taught me a few tricks to handle the Browsers of the world. What I didn't tell you was that he almost lost the capacity to father children while he was teaching me. I'm a fast learner, Jack. Very fast.''

The glint of laughter in his eyes told her she'd won. This time.

At precisely one o'clock, she unlocked the Chevy.

Dressed once more in the tailored tunic and skirt that served as her uniform, Angela waited beside the car while Jack tossed the little notebook computer on the back seat. It joined the paper sacks holding the meager possessions they'd accumulated during their stay in the cabin.

He slammed the rear door and took a last look around the clearing. The wind ruffled his black hair and put blades of color in his cheeks. He'd changed into his charcoal-gray suit and a blue shirt he'd purchased during their quick shopping expedition, but she knew him too well now to be taken in by that conservative executive image. Under that pale blue shirt and tailored suit beat the heart of a predator.

It was time to bag their prey.

Angela slid into the driver's seat, buckled her safety belt and inserted the key into the ignition. While Jack strapped himself in beside her, she checked her watch a final time.

''If Mother's communication net is working—and it hasn't been known to fail yet—the entire Paretti clan will start their engines in five seconds. Four. Three. Two. One.''

She twisted the key and flashed Jack another grin. ''Hang on. This is going to be a ride you won't ever forget.''

He believed her. He could remember being in some

pretty tight situations before this one. He'd jumped out of a couple of planes he hadn't really wanted to leave, and swum ashore in a few countries he never wanted to return to. But he couldn't remember his hair actually standing on end before Angela hit the gas and spun the Chevy in a three-hundred-and-sixty-degree turn to test its responsiveness.

Their prearranged police escort fell in as soon as the Chevy turned onto the state road. Belatedly Jack realized that providing Angela Paretti with a police escort was like giving a thief a license to steal. Once they gained the controlled-access six-lane highway leading into the city, the speedometer rarely dropped below eighty.

Just outside the Washington, D.C., Beltway, Jack noticed that they'd picked up additional protection. An entire fleet of silver stretch limousines and dark green trucks emblazoned with Giancarlo's Fine Italian Pastries on the side panels had taken up strategic positions on overpasses and exit ramps. No one was going to take any potshots or drop rocks on their windshield as they passed, Angela informed Jack cheerfully.

The Paretti family was taking care of its own.

# Chapter 14

Once inside the Beltway, the motorcade avoided D.C.'s main thoroughfares and whipped through back streets. Tires whined in fast, tight turns, and more than one passerby turned to stare at the fast-moving parade of police cars and limos and bakery trucks.

At a quarter to two, Angela pulled up at the security checkpoint that guarded the underground parking lot of the Capitol. Moments later, the Chevy whizzed into the senator's assigned slot, where Manny Ramirez and Ed Winters stood waiting.

"No trouble?" the special agent asked, his face tight.

"None," Jack replied, raking a hand through hair he suspected was still standing straight up. "How about at your end?"

Manny patted his pocket. "The U.S. magistrate signed warrants for search and seizure of any and all documents related to the HealthMark investigation and for the arrest of one Marc Green."

"Good!"

"Looks like our case is about to bust wide open," the agent said, relief and regret coloring his voice. "Federal marshals in six states will be knocking on a whole bunch of doors in less than an hour."

Jack held out his hand. "You've done a hell of a job, Ramirez."

Their hard, tight handshake came as close as anything could have to expressing the bond forged by their months of intensive labor and increasing tension.

"Yeah, well, I'd say we make a pretty good team." Jack's brief smile included Angela and Ed Winters. "I'd say we all do."

Winters hitched up his belt. "I'll feel more like I've contributed to this team after we confront Green. I don't know about your big medical fraud investigation, but the mayor's chomping at the bit to announce a break in the bridge shooting. It's made our citizens just a little nervous, you understand?"

The detective's teeth showed white in the dim light. "Of course, the fact that Senator Claiborne's senior aide might be a prime suspect has only added to the mayor's impatience."

"If your boss thinks he's going to score some political points off this," Angela retorted, stabbing at the elevator button, "he doesn't know the senator."

"If Marc Green blinks, or even breathes the wrong way," Jack said softly, "there might not be enough left of him for anyone to score points off, political or otherwise. Let's go."

Angela led the way. Avoiding the echoing rotunda crowded with the usual groups of tourists, she took the three men into the Senate chamber, then up the private staircase that led directly to Henry Claiborne's office.

A cautious peek showed that the senator was alone, and that the solid oak door between his inner sanctum and the outer offices was firmly shut.

He rose at their entrance. His eyes glinting like chips of pale blue ice, he nodded to Angela and the two investigators, then fixed his gaze on Jack's face.

"You want to tell me what this is all about, son?" he asked, keeping his voice low. "Angela said only that we had to talk, privately. Without any of my staff present."

"It might be easier to show you instead of tell you."

Jack opened the dog-eared copy of Senate Bill 693 on the conference table to the next-to-the-last page, where a single small paragraph was circled in red. Placing the bound bill on the conference table, he laid a sheet of paper with neat columns of figures next to it. With an economy of words, he explained his calculations.

As the senator took in the differing bottom lines, a tide of red climbed up the back of his neck and heated his face, until his carroty mustache lost its startling contrast to his skin.

"Are you sure about these numbers?"

"No. They're just an estimate. A very conservative estimate. In my opinion, the actual numbers are probably higher."

Obviously shaken, the senator swiped a palm across his shiny crown. Angela's heart ached at the tremor in his hand.

"I should've caught that clause," he muttered to himself. "Damn, I should've caught it. Maybe I'm gettin' a mite too old and too tired for this business."

Jowls flapping, he gave himself a little shake. His glance flicked to Ramirez, then centered on Jack.

"Do you boys still think that I'm in HealthMark's pocket? That I inserted that language deliberately?"

"No," Jack replied. "But we have an idea who did."

As he laid out the bare facts they'd gathered about Marc Green, the ruddy color in the senator's face deepened. When Manny added that the HealthMark PR executive who'd spent two weeks on a cruise ship with Marc had just been picked up for questioning, the legislator's mustache twitched like a startled squirrel's tail.

"Well," he said after a long, weighty pause, "I do believe it's time we treed us a coon."

Striding to his desk, he pressed the intercom button.

"Yes, sir?" Marc Green's voice sounded reedy and thin over the intercom.

"Bring in the history file on the medical reform bill, would you? I want to review it."

"Now? But the—"

"Now."

Her heart pumping, Angela moved to one side of the room with Jack and the two investigators. The senator settled in his chair and linked his hands over his stomach.

Behind him, tall windows framed a spectacular view of the long, rectangular Mall, lined on either side by the eclectic group of buildings that formed the Smithsonian Institution. At the far end of the Mall, the Washington Monument stood silhouetted against the gray February sky like a solitary sentry. The majestic vista formed a fitting backdrop, Angela thought, for the drama that was about to unfold.

It seemed like an eternity to her, but no doubt was only a few moments, until the door to the outer office opened and Marc Green strode in. She strained to detect some sign of nervousness in the aide's voice or appearance but couldn't find one. Every strand of his thinning sandy hair was neatly combed. His woven brown leather suspenders held up sharp, creased navy trousers. His white shirt showed nothing that even faintly resembled a perspiration stain.

He was halfway across the plush red carpet before he noticed her and Jack and the others. He stopped abruptly, his nostrils flaring. The thick file in his hand shook noticeably for an instant.

Then, incredibly, he smiled.

It was a tight, thin smile. Just enough to fan the fury Angela had banked during the past hours into a hot, searing flame.

"You're here early, Angela, you and Dr. Merritt. I should've known you'd cut considerable time off your ETA in Tony's Corvette."

Shaking with the force of her anger, Angela stepped forward. "I didn't drive Tony's Vette in, Marc."

His gaze flickered for an instant, then settled on Manny Ramirez and Ed Winters. "No, I don't suppose you could fit everyone in the Vette. Are you gentlemen all here to listen to Dr. Merritt's testimony?"

A small, feral light gleamed in Jack's eyes as he sauntered forward. "No, as a matter of fact, they're not. This is Special Agent Ramirez from the Miami office of the Food and Drug Administration, and Detective Winters from the Washington, D.C., Metropolitan Police. They're here to talk to you, Green."

The blood drained from the staffer's face, but he managed to put on a good front. Sandy brows lifting, he turned to his boss.

"What's this all about, Senator?"

Coon Dog Claiborne steepled his fingers over his

stomach. From beneath his hooded lids, the sharp, cutting lasers of his pale blue eyes lanced into his aide.

"Well, sir, I think you'd better tell us. In the process, maybe you'd better tell me about this little two-week cruise you took last year, compliments of HealthMark, Incorporated."

For one wild instant, Angela thought Marc might bolt. His face paper white, he jerked a look over his shoulder at the door.

"Try it, Green," Jack murmured with lethal softness. "Do me a favor and try it."

To Angela's intense disappointment, Marc didn't try anything. Dammit! She wanted to see him pounded into the carpet! She wanted to help with the pounding!

Her disappointment vaulted into total disgust when the staffer placed the thick file on the senator's desk, drew himself up to blade-stiffness and stonily faced his boss.

"I want to speak to an attorney."

"You can call one from downtown," Manny Ramirez informed him.

Scooping up the thick file, he gave the staffer a smile that held all the warmth of a shark closing in on its next meal.

"I'm obligated to advise you of your rights according to the Miranda ruling, Mr. Green. You're familiar with Miranda, aren't you?"

As she listened to the special agent reading a rigid, unspeaking Marc his rights, Angela told herself that she *might* pity him when they discovered what had driven him to such desperate acts. She *might* even forgive him. Someday. But when Manny and Ed Winters handcuffed Marc and hustled him past an openmouthed staff, she felt only a fierce satisfaction that his exit from the corridors of power was so public and so humiliating.

Her exultation took an abrupt downward spiral when she turned and caught sight of her boss. Shoulders slumped, mustache drooping, he watched his senior aide being led away.

"I should have seen it," he muttered again.

Not forty minutes later, the senator's exclamation bounced off the paneled office walls.

"Those bastards!"

His color erupted from bright red into purple. Clasping his hands behind his back, he pounded a track in front of his desk.

"They promised Marc Green my seat?" Disbelief reverberated through every booming word. "Those bastards at HealthMark promised Marc Green my Senate seat?"

From across the expanse of red carpet, Jack caught Angela's eyes. The glint in their brown depths told him that she, too, had noted her boss's transformation. The man whose hand had trembled and whose shoulders had slumped such a short time ago might never have existed. One phone call from Ramirez had relit the fires in his heart.

"According to Manny's contact in the FBI," Jack informed the thoroughly agitated legislator, "Ms. Palmer is as anxious to cop a plea as the hit man Uncle Guido delivered to the police last night. She, too, is spilling her guts. Literally. She threw up all over the police interview room."

"Good!" Angela interjected. She sincerely hoped the unknown Ms. Palmer stayed sick for a long, long time.

"She admitted that she dangled the tantalizing offe

of HealthMark's support if Green decided to run in the next election as your replacement. Evidently he jumped at the offer.''

"My replacement!" the senator thundered. "As if he could replace me!"

"Evidently HealthMark wanted someone in this office who'd be more sympathetic to their interests.''

Angela's "Ahem" matched the legislator's harrumph in both volume and tone. Smiling, Jack shared the rest of the details an ecstatic Manny had just relayed.

"By the time you heard about my audits and invited me to Washington, Green was in so deep with HealthMark, he couldn't have dug himself out with a bulldozer. We don't know yet if someone at HealthMark was behind his actions or if he decided on his own to eliminate the source of the audits before the results were released to the public. But we will.''

That set the senator off again. Mustache twitching in outrage, he blustered for several minutes about vipers and polecats and several more unpleasant life-forms indigenous to Washington, D.C. When his face turned bright purple again, Angela crossed to the water carafe on the console behind his desk.

"Here." She pushed a glass of water into his hand. "You'd better calm down before you blow a gasket.''

While he took a long, gulping swallow, she flicked a quick glance at the clock above the door.

"The hearing's scheduled to begin in ten minutes. Do you want to delay it a while longer, just to give yourself time to get over the shock?''

The senator thumped the glass down on his desk. "It will be a cold day in hell, missy, a *very* cold day in hell, before I let the likes of Marc Green disrupt the process of this august body.''

Anchoring both hands on the lapels of his white suit, he lifted his chin and pulled his dignity around him like a cloak.

"Well, sir, are you ready for your first appearance before a duly constituted committee of the United States Congress?"

"As ready as I'll ever be, Senator."

Abandoning his lofty pose, the legislator gave his witness a piece of well-meant advice. "Some folks feel that testifying before the Congress is a daunting experience. Just answer the questions to the best of your ability, son, and leave the rest to me."

Jack's glinting gaze settled on Angela. "I just rode in from Maryland with your driver and a police escort, Senator. Testifying before a congressional subcommittee can't begin to compare with that experience."

Unsure whether she'd just been flattered or insulted, Angela preceded the two men out the door. Her boss used the brief underground monorail ride to the Russell Office Building, where the Senate conducted most of its day-to-day business, to fill Jack in on the other committee members. With a final slap on the back, he left his star witness at the entrance to the committee room and headed for the caucus room behind it.

Flashing her ID at the usher, Angela escorted Jack into the drab, functional chamber. A gathering crowd of spectators filed into rows of seats separated from the witness table by an oak rail. Bristling with microphones, the witness table faced the banked platforms where the Senators would seat themselves. A single printed placard sat on the table, indicating Jack's seat.

He'd be alone at that table, facing an entire battery of senators. Suddenly, unaccountably nervous on his behalf, Angela stopped at the rail.

"You're the only one scheduled to testify this afternoon. I hope it doesn't get too lonely at that table."

"Where will you be?"

"Right behind you."

His smile warmed her to the tips of her toes. "I won't be lonely."

A flurry of aides scuttled out of the caucus room, telling Angela that the hearings were about to commence. She bit her lip, her fluttery tension mounting by the second.

Most of the hearings she'd attended in this room she could only have described as stultifying. She'd listened to incredibly verbose witnesses read dry prepared statements that had half the room nodding off and the other half doodling on every available scrap of paper.

On a few memorable occasions, however, she'd witnessed some real bloodbaths. Once, a four-star general had left the room with the tips of his ears burning and his jaw locked so tight Angela was sure it would crack. Several industrialists had walked out of this chamber to face a barrage of media questions and demands for their resignations. Recently, a well-known rock star testifying about pornography in the arts had lost every shred of professional poise and broken down in tears.

Angela didn't want Jack reduced to tears, or even to burning ear tips. She hesitated, then offered the only encouragement she could.

"Good luck."

"Thanks."

He didn't look the least bit nervous, she thought enviously. She was quivering inside on his behalf, and he hadn't even worked up a damp palm.

She took her seat, remembering how she'd derided Jack after the bridge incident for the fact that he appeared so calm and in control. How she'd accused him of lacking basic human emotions, like a number of his bean-counter peers she and her family had had to deal with.

Now, Angela only wished she possessed a tenth of his poise and control. Shoving her hands into her pockets again to keep from chewing on her nails, she waited for the proceedings to commence.

Fifteen minutes into the hearing, Angela stopped worrying and started enjoying herself as much as the senator and Jack obviously were.

They made worthy opponents, she thought wryly. Her boss's style tended toward the flamboyant, and his circuitous, often meandering questions carried all kinds of traps for the unwary. By contrast, Jack responded with short, straightforward answers and handled himself with the utter confidence of a vice president and chief financial officer.

Seated directly behind him, Angela felt the different layers of lust and love that this man generated in her take on a deeper texture. Respect added a richness to the slowly forming tapestry of her emotions. Admiration wove its way through each separate strand of feeling.

He sat easily in the oak witness chair, his broad shoulders square and his every movement assured. Most of the questions he answered from memory. About the system of audits he'd instituted at Children's. About the various tasks he'd measured. About the deviations from the statistical norm he'd noticed and corrected.

As Angela had known he would, the senator eventually zeroed in on the audit Jack had conducted on prescriptions written for the growth hormone Gromorphin.

In response to his questions, Jack laid the bare facts on the table. Yes, he'd conducted an audit of prescriptions written for that particular drug. Yes, he'd discovered that certain physicians had written a percentage of prescriptions that deviated significantly from any expected norm, given their caseloads and previous histories.

Murmurs and exclamations arose from the crowd of spectators as Jack calmly related the suspicions that had led to a four-month investigation of Gromorphin's distributor, HealthMark, Incorporated.

"The same company," the senator announced to the thunderstruck listeners, "that I have reason to believe corrupted a member of my own staff. A member of my own staff!"

With the consummate showmanship of a career politician, Henry Claiborne played to his crowd. His voice quivering with indignation, he detailed his grave, yes, grave reservations about the unbridled power of companies such as HealthMark. Companies with so many fingers in the health care pie that only the most carefully crafted government oversight could curb them. Companies that contributed to the escalating costs that drove health care out of reach for too many, far too many, of this nation's citizens. Pounding his fist on his desk, he ended with a resounding call for medical reform that won a burst of applause from all listeners.

Except Jack.

And Angela.

For the first time, she wasn't swayed by her boss's fervent call to arms or by her family's bitter experiences. This time, she listened to Jack's voice. Calm. Steady. Rational.

He didn't argue. He didn't dispute the issues involved. As he had the night before with Angela, he simply fed the issues back to the committee from a different perspective.

Smoothly, persuasively, succinctly, he made a convincing case for less government control, instead of more. For a simple set of norms that would allow the medical community the flexibility they needed to operate, while still providing a yardstick to measure acceptable performance.

When he finished, the audience didn't burst into applause, but a swell of comments and murmurs of approval filled the hearing room. Senator Claiborne slouched in his high-backed chair, twirling one tip of his mustache between his fingers. For long, moments, his gaze held Jack's.

"Well, sir, you raise some interestin' points. Most interestin'. Perhaps we should take another look at one or two provisions in this bill."

"More than one or two, Senator."

The legislator smiled and placed a hand over the microphone directly in front of him. In a mumbled aside, he consulted with his colleagues. When he faced Jack again, he wore the fox-in-the-henhouse expression Angela knew all too well.

"The members of this committee would value your input on any revisions, Dr. Merritt."

Jack's voice held only a hint of a drawl. "It would be my pleasure to provide it, Senator."

"Would you consider acting as an ad hoc advisor to this committee? As such, we'd require you to meet with us at least once or twice a month for the near future."

Angela slapped a hand over her mouth to muffle her involuntary laughter. The old reprobate! He'd led his sacrificial goat to the altar and gotten a swift butt in the hindquarters for his efforts. Now, he was trying to entice the former victim into joining his ranks.

Leaping excitement swiftly overtook Angela's mirth. Her crafty boss was also offering both her and Jack the chance to take their short, tumultuous relationship to the next plane.

In the brief time they'd known each other, she and Jack hadn't allowed themselves to think beyond the immediate danger. Certainly not beyond this hearing. They hadn't had time to sort through their feelings. To talk about a future. The idea that Jack might return to Washington on a regular basis for the foreseeable future sent a wave of joy flooding through her.

They could explore this shimmering, sensual, heady sensation that verged on the edge of something wonderful.

They could discover what each liked to eat, in addition to fresh baked cannoli and *fettuccine con salsa di noci.*

They could break the NASCAR record for fast turnarounds!

With all her heart, she urged Jack to say yes.

"I'm honored," he began.

The senator held up a palm. "I know this is quite an imposition, sir, given your many responsibilities in Atlanta. We'll do everything we can to make your trips to Washington as productive as possible."

His blue eyes twinkled as his gaze slid past Jack's shoulder and settled on Angela.

"You can trust my staff to see to your needs."

Without so much as a backward glance, Jack took him up on his offer. "I accept."

# Chapter 15

"Uh-oh!"

Angela brought Gus's Chevy to a stop in the middle of a tree-lined Baltimore street. Gripping the steering wheel with both hands, she peered through the deepening twilight at the vehicles jammed bumper to bumper along both curbs outside her parents' house.

Their home, she amended silently. She still had trouble thinking of this elegantly restored flat-fronted row dwelling in Baltimore's famed Little Italy district as home. Soon after Tony's accident, her parents had sold the cheerfully shabby house they'd lived in for thirty years and moved into a tiny apartment. Despite their protests, Tony had purchased this place for them within a month of opening his first auto parts store. He was now franchised in twelve states and had repaid his parents twice over for every penny they'd put toward his medical expenses, but he, like Angela, still regretted the loss of their old house.

Tony was here tonight, Angela saw. His Corvette sat in the driveway, blocked in by a green-and-tan bakery van. Two silver limos were parked nose-to-nose in front of the house. Family cars of every color and style spilled onto the side streets that led to the Harborplace, only a few blocks away. Angela eyed the congested street with a combination of resignation and dismay.

"Mother must have activated the net. It looks as though half the family's here."

"Only half?"

The wry amusement in Jack's voice drew her gaze to his shadowed face.

"You don't have to do this."

"Stop worrying, Angela. I want to meet your family."

"I want you to meet them, too," she muttered. "Just not all at once. Their sheer numbers can be a bit…overpowering."

"Stop worrying."

"Right."

She eased the Chevy into gear and wedged it into a narrow space between a street lamp and a trash can. Grabbing her purse, she joined Jack on the sidewalk. The sounds of lively laughter and animated conversation carried from the jammed house, punctuated at intervals by the soaring, soulful voice of a tenor.

"Pavarotti or Caruso?" Jack inquired, cocking his head to catch the strains of the familiar ballad.

"Neither. That's my cousin Michael. He's a pharmacist by day, and star of Hagerstown Little Theater by night."

"He's good. Very good."

"Wait until he's downed a few more glasses of vino. Then he's not only good, he's loud. Very loud." She slung her purse over her shoulder. ''Are you sure you're ready for this?''

''Lead the way.''

He was so calm, Angela thought enviously as she weaved though the parked cars. So amazingly in control and—her mouth curved in a rueful smile—so very un-Italian.

A half pace behind her, Jack surreptitiously swiped his palms down the sides of his leg. He couldn't remember the last time he'd been so damned nervous!

He hadn't lied when he told Angela he was looking forward to meeting her family. He'd spent enough boyhood years in his grandfather's empty, echoing house to harbor hopes for a large and lively family of his own someday. Those hopes hadn't come to fruition with his former wife, and Jack hadn't had the time or the inclination to pursue them since his divorce.

He'd been thinking about large, boisterous families for the past few days, however. Thinking hard. Whenever his mind wasn't consumed by worry about Angela's safety, it had been consumed by Angela herself. He'd never met anyone with her passion for life, and he couldn't think of anyone he'd rather share that life with.

He knew damn well he'd rushed her. Knew that he'd pushed her into his arms, despite his promise to let her name the time and the place. The rules of civilized behavior told Jack he should back off, give her time to deal with the tangled emotions of the past few days. But the primal male in him wanted to stake his claim now. Tonight. In front of her entire family. Or half of them, anyway. As he mounted the front steps, he tried to visualize her family's reaction to such a claim.

Tony, he could handle. Maybe.

Uncle Guido, he wasn't as sure of. The semiretired counterfeiter seemed to have some well-placed connections.

Angela's father was as yet an unknown quantity.

But it was her mother who worried Jack the most. He hadn't forgotten Ed Winters's near panic at the thought of another call from Maria Paretti. Or the senator's alarmed expression when he'd instructed his driver to call home. If Angela's mother could put two such strong personalities into a quake, she had to be a formidable woman.

She was. Formidable and grim-faced.

She appeared the moment Jack and Angela stepped into a foyer filled with the mouth-watering aroma of garlicky lasagna and the rousing strains of Cousin Michael in full voice. "Angela!" she declared, raising her clasped hands to the ceiling in prayerful thanksgiving. "At last you come home!"

Angela gave the black-clad mustachioed woman a tight hug and a hearty kiss on each cheek. "Hello, Aunt Rose."

Instant, cowardly relief speared through Jack.

"This is Jack Merritt, Aunt Rose. You talked to him last night...or I guess it was this morning."

"I remember." Rose Paretti's three chins folded one into the other as she looked Jack up and down. "Divorced. Thirty-six. No children. I don't know about this one, *carina.*"

Laughing, Angela hooked her arm through Jack's. "He came for wine, Aunt Rose. And lasagna. And to meet everyone involved in our adventure before he has to go back to Atlanta. That's all."

"You'd better make sure he meets your mother first," Rose warned ominously. "She's in the kitchen."

"We'll go right there."

Despite Angela's assurances, it took some time to work their way through the crowd of adults, scampering children, crawling toddlers and noisy babies filling the front rooms. As he passed through the talking, gesticulating throng, Jack met Cousin Teresa. He renewed his acquaintance with her husband, Gus. He shook hands with Dominic, who urged Jack to try the *spaghetti alle vongole* the next time Angela brought him to the restaurant. He accepted a brimming glass of red wine from Leonard, whose mother, Helen, modestly acknowledged that she was the artist who'd baked the cannoli her niece had offered Jack on the Fourteenth Street Bridge.

Juggling the glass of wine and a slice of melon wrapped in prosciutto that someone—Michael's mother, Julia, he thought—had pressed on him, he followed in Angela's wake. Halfway down a narrow hall, his guide caught sight of Tony coming toward them. With a cry of joy, she threw herself at him. Tony's bad leg buckled under the force of her exuberant greeting and he staggered back a pace or two, but his arms went around her and he hugged her as fiercely as she hugged him.

"Did you hear about Marc Green?" she asked breathlessly.

"I heard. He'd better sleep with one eye open for a while. A long while."

Throwing a grin over her shoulder, Angela elaborated for Jack's benefit. "A number of Uncle Guido's, er, former business associates are behind bars."

Tony acknowledged his presence with a neutral nod. When he released his sister and held out his hand, Jack didn't make the mistake of thinking that he was offering friendship. Not yet. He wouldn't, until he knew exactly how things stood between his sister and the stranger who'd plunged her into danger.

With a small smile, Jack slipped his hand into his pocket and passed the other man the snub-nosed revolver. Tony palmed the weapon into his own pocket.

"I'd better go lock this away. Mom's in the kitchen."

"We're on our way," Angela assured him.

The mouth-watering aroma of garlic and spicy, bubbling lasagna grew thicker with each step. When Jack finally entered the mobbed kitchen, a half step behind Angela, a rush of oven-baked heat enveloped him. Wishing he'd taken the time to shed his suit coat, he felt a fine sweat film his forehead.

"Hello, Mamma."

At Angela's call, a tiny, delicate woman threw up her hands and gave a joyous shriek. Flying across the kitchen, she wrapped her daughter in a teary hug, kissed her, patted her cheeks and her chin several times, then kissed her again. When she finally released a laughing, equally teary Angela and turned to Jack, he felt the magnetic pull of her limpid brown eyes.

Her olive-toned skin was as lustrous as her daughter's, he noted, and it was immediately obvious which parent had given Angela her fine bone structure. Tilting her head, Maria Paretti searched his face for long moments. What she read there, he had no idea, but a Mona Lisa-like smile lifted the corners of her lips. Releasing her daughter, she tucked her arm through Jack's and pulled him toward a huge oval kitchen table.

"Tony told us about this business with that *bastardo* at the senator's office. I want to know every detail. Every one. After you eat. Sit down. Both of you, sit down."

More than a little stunned, Jack sat. This was the

woman who set grown men to trembling with a single phone call? This luminous, smiling Madonna was the master manipulator who kept tabs on her family via a voice-activated communications net that rivaled the military's?

Across the table, Angela knuckled the curly head of a gurgling toddler and winked at Jack.

"Don't breathe easy yet. Your trial by fire is just beginning. Mother's favorite tactic is to stuff her unsuspecting victims to the bursting point, then threaten them with more food unless they tell her everything she wants to know. And I'm not talking about Marc Green. You won't have any secrets when you leave here, Jack. None!"

Confident of his abilities to hold his own against the charming, vivacious woman who set a mountain of crusty lasagna in front of him, Jack picked up a fork and dug in.

He soon learned his mistake.

Before he'd made a noticeable dent in the mountain, Maria Paretti had elicited his occupation, his family background, the precise state of his health, and the interesting information that, no, he wasn't Catholic, but he *had* visited the Vatican on a long-ago shore leave.

Wisely Jack omitted any reference to the fact that he and his two buddies had been decidedly worse for their wine when they decided to get the pope's personal blessing. He also didn't mention that the three U.S. sailors had made it only as far as the first entry point before two large and unamused Swiss Guards turned them over to the civilian authorities.

Luckily, the arrival of two men saved Jack from further inquisition. One was a shorter, stockier, older edition of Tony, the other a bandy-legged, silver-haired gnome with a gold eyetooth.

"Pop! Uncle Guido!"

Jack rose as the gray-haired, barrel-chested Anthony Paretti, Sr., enveloped his daughter in a bone-crunching bear hug. While she exchanged a similar greeting with her uncle, her father gripped Jack's hand with the confidence and strength of a man who'd spent his entire adult life working as a stevedore on Baltimore's docks.

"You're welcome in our home."

"Thank you."

"Tony says you took care of our Angela."

Her little huff warned Jack to tread lightly. "She does a pretty good job of taking care of herself."

"Yes, she does." The weathered lines at the corners of her father's eyes folded into a smile. "Of course, we'll never convince her mother of that."

"Not in this lifetime, anyway," Maria Paretti put in complacently from across the kitchen.

Groaning, Angela introduced her great-uncle.

"Thanks for the loan of the cabin," Jack said sincerely. "And for the assistance your, ah, associates gave the police."

In a classic Paretti gesture, Uncle Guido waved a hand through the air.

"Angela's family," he said simply. "We take care of family."

Three hours later, Angela turned down her parents' offer of the spare bedrooms and Tony's offer of his Vette. Promising to deliver Gus's dark green Chevy to the lot the next morning, she escaped with the excuses that she had to make arrangements for the senator's transportation—and that Jack had to finalize his own travel plans.

"When do you have to fly home to Atlanta?" she asked as they walked to the car, confronting the issue head-on.

"Tomorrow morning, I suppose," Jack said slowly. "I should be there when the media starts clamoring for details of the investigation."

Children's Hospital would be at the center of the storm, he knew, because of his involvement...and that of his best friend, Philip. Jack had put in a quick call to his boss from the senator's office. He'd explained about the investigation and warned that several of the hospital's consulting physicians and suppliers were implicated.

Then he'd called Philip. Although his friend had been an integral part of the investigative team since the night Jack confronted him with the initial audit results, the physician would still have to face the censure of his associates and colleagues for the kickbacks he'd accepted. Jack didn't want Philip and his wife to face them alone.

"Tomorrow, huh?" Angela asked softly.

As she backed the Chevy onto the street and pointed it toward the Washington-Baltimore Expressway, she struggled to accept the idea of Jack leaving so soon. She understood the heavy responsibilities and obligations that pulled at him. She respected his loyalty to his friend. She reminded herself that he'd return within a week, two at most.

The two weeks loomed ahead of her as dark and empty as the toll road.

Jack stretched an arm across the back of her seat and kneaded the back of her neck. His touch was gentle, and blatantly possessive. Her pulse leaped in response. Arching her neck under the erotic massage, she let the pleasure of his touch seep through her.

"I have to go home, Angela," he said quietly. "But I'll be back. Soon."

The Chevy ate up the pavement. They sat silent for some time, each lost in their own thoughts. When the cutoff for Annapolis and Uncle Guido's cabin flashed by, Jack roused enough to ask where they were going.

"My place," Angela told him.

His fingers didn't cease their slow, sensual movement. "Does it have a bed?"

"Of course it has a bed."

"A real bed? Not one of those narrow shelf things? Not that I mind your bottom bumping and grinding into me all night, you understand. I'm just wondering."

"It's king-size," she assured him solemnly.

"King-size?" His fingers stroked her neck. "How long will it take to get to your place?"

"From here, it would take most people another half hour. I put our ETA at twenty minutes."

"Go for it."

They made it in seventeen. Retrieving the paper sacks containing their purchased possessions from the back seat, Jack followed Angela into the rambling three-story brownstone, just a few blocks north of the Capitol. Her apartment consisted of three airy, high-ceilinged rooms decorated with drooping ferns, bookshelves crammed with textbooks, framed prints from the Smithsonian and a scattering of sneakers and athletic sweats she hadn't had time to put away.

Jack grinned at the orange-and-purple-striped running shoes she scooped up with the sweats.

"Nice shoes."

"A girl's gotta make a statement," she replied with a toss of her hair. "Even in a chauffeur's uniform. Especially in a chauffeur's uniform."

Dumping the gear behind the couch, she turned to find Jack examining the collage of framed photographs on the top shelf of the bookcase. He picked up one of Tony, flushed and triumphant as he held aloft a silver trophy. A ponytailed, grease-stained Angela grinned gleefully at his side.

"How old were you here?"

"Fifteen. I'd just gotten my learner's permit the week before, and Tony had let me drive a test lap. He sweated the whole way around the track."

"I can sympathize with him," Jack murmured, replacing the photograph. He closed the distance between them and speared both hands through the hair at her temples. Tilting her face to his, he smiled down at her.

"Thanks for introducing me to your family, Angela."

She covered his hands with hers. "I wanted you to meet them. Not all of them at once, but... Well, they're who I am. If we're going to see each other when you come back to Washington..."

"We're going to see each other."

"Then you needed to know I come fully equipped with family, friends, an assortment of sneakers...and a spotless driving record," she tacked on. "Think you can learn to trust my driving enough to stop stomping your foot against the floor mats, Dr. Merritt?"

"I can try, Ms. Paretti." He brushed his mouth over hers. "Think you can teach me to thread a car through an opening the size of a lug nut?"

"I can try." Grinning, she slid her arms around his neck. "Not tonight, though."

"No, not tonight."

His mouth came down on hers, heavy and hungry.

Angela melted into him. They had tonight, she told herself fiercely. And tomorrow, until his flight left. And the days and weeks he'd spend in Washington during the months to come. They had time to let the passion that shimmered between them develop into the kind of enduring love she wanted with this man. The kind of love her parents felt for each other. The kind the senator and Lilly had discovered. She didn't need to feel this sense of panic at the thought of him leaving tomorrow.

But she did. She did.

Her fingers trembled as she yanked at the buttons on his shirt. Jack caught her urgency. His mouth slanted over hers. His hands slid down her back to shape her hips. He brought her against him, and Angela's breath caught as she arched against his hardness. When he scooped her up with the same ease with which she'd snatched up her sweats a few moments ago and headed for the bedroom, the breath left her body completely.

Holding her mouth with his, he set her on her feet and went to work on her clothes. She tugged at his with the same eager hands.

"You're so beautiful," he murmured, shaping her breasts with his palms. "All creamy and soft and sweet, like a rich, chewy praline."

She speared her fingers through the pelt of dark hair on his chest. "You're not so bad yourself. For a number-crunching VP, you strip down pretty good."

She was aching and on fire when they tumbled to the bed in a whirl of greedy kisses and tangled limbs. Angela wrapped her legs around his, desperate for the feel of his strength surging into her.

"Easy, sweetheart," Jack murmured against the fevered skin of her neck. "We'll take it slow and sweet.

We've got all night, and a king-size bed. I want to remember every minute of this.''

"You'll remember every minute," she promised, sliding her palm down his belly. "You will."

Angela didn't want easy. She didn't want slow. She wanted to leave her scent all over Jack, and his in every crevice of her body.

He filled her hand. Hot. Satiny. As sleek and as hard as a smooth-bore piston.

She stroked him with the exquisite care she'd give a high-performance engine. Deliberately, she primed him. Fiercely, she exulted as his breath grew more ragged in her ear.

Then he reversed positions and his fingers found the tight center of sensation between her legs. His touch set off small spirals of pleasure. When he bent his body and brought his mouth down to her breast, the spirals spun into searing, liquid delight.

"Now, Jack." She arched her back, groaning. "I choose now. Here! Ooooh!"

With a growl of pleasure, he surged into her. Almost instantly, her body spasmed around him. Her long, drawn-out moan escalated into a wild cry that drove him straight over the edge.

Angela awoke the next morning the same way she always did. Reluctantly. Grudgingly.

Wincing at the sunlight that streamed through the fanlights above the tall bedroom windows, she tugged the tangled covers over her head. Instantly, warmth and the lingering scent of love surrounded her. More slowly, the realization that she was alone in the warm, dark cocoon penetrated her consciousness.

Frowning, she pushed her head out of the covers.

There were no signs of Jack in the bedroom, and no sound coming from any of the other rooms. A heavy stillness hung over the apartment, disturbed only by the faint rumble of early rush-hour traffic outside.

Her frown deepening, Angela shoved the covers aside and swung out of bed. Grabbing the maroon-and-gold Washington Redskins T-shirt she used as a sleepshirt from the chair beside the bed, she slipped it on and padded barefoot into the living room.

Showered, shaved and fully dressed, Jack was ensconced in the apartment's only comfortable armchair, perusing the newspaper. Ruefully Angela realized that she'd slept right through his morning ritual…and that he'd let her. They'd have to work on their morning routines, she decided. The next time she shared a bed with Jack Merritt, she wanted to wake up in his arms.

He glanced up at her entrance, and her heart thumped painfully at the smile that formed in his eyes. It was the one he'd given her at the airport the first time they met, a potent combination of admiration and masculine appreciation that made her forget her unbrushed hair and unwashed face.

Her bare toes curling with pleasure, she returned the smile. "Morning."

"Good morning."

The newspaper rustled as he dropped it and rose to greet her with more than words. Angela crossed one foot over the other as he brushed the tangled strands from her forehead. Just the touch of his hand on her skin brought back instant, erotic memories of the night before.

"I poked around in the kitchen," he told her. "I was going to serve you breakfast in bed before I left, but all

I could find was a box of stale crackers and some mineral water.''

Angela's dreamy pleasure faded abruptly at the reminder of his imminent departure. Hiding her dismay, she dismissed her empty cupboards with an airy wave. ''I usually eat out. What time is your flight?''

He glanced at his watch. ''In an hour. It was the only flight to Atlanta today available on this short notice.''

''I'd better get dressed, then.''

He caught her arm, his fingers warm on her bare skin. ''You've got the senator to take care of. I'll call a cab.''

Angela summoned a grin. ''No way, Merritt. The senator said his staff would take care of all your needs when you're here, remember? I'll get you to the airport, and I guarantee we won't get stuck on the bridge this time.''

Driving against the rush-hour traffic streaming into the city, Angela made excellent time to the airport.

Tires screeching, she pulled into the same spot in front of the Delta terminal where she'd parked illegally and waited for Jack just a few days ago. Ignoring the yellow stripe on the curb and the No Parking signs posted every ten feet, she switched off the ignition.

A chill February wind knifed through her purple suede jacket as she joined Jack on the sidewalk. The matching knee-length suede skirt swirled in the breeze. Shivering, she burrowed into Jack's arms.

His kiss promised everything he'd whispered to her last night. When he raised his head, his gray eyes confirmed that promise.

''I don't want any goodbyes between us. Ever. I'll be back, Angela. Soon.''

She smiled. ''I'll be waiting.''

# Chapter 16

Jack took exactly two steps into the terminal, then stopped abruptly.

Passengers shot him disgruntled looks as they side-stepped around his unmoving form. Jack ignored their mumbled comments. He ignored the flashing notice on the huge arrival-and-departure board that indicated that his flight was in the process of boarding. He ignored everything but the single thought that drummed through his head.

What was he doing?

What the hell was he doing?

He'd walked away from his cold, uncaring grandfather and never looked back. Against his ex-wife's wishes, he'd accepted the position at Children's and watched her walk away from their marriage. Now, like a fool, he was walking away from Angela.

He was only leaving for a few weeks, his logical, rational mind asserted. He'd be back. He'd promised her that he'd be back, and he would. Within a week or two, three at most.

Jack stood stock-still for another moment or two, thinking about those weeks. Then he spun on one heel and raced for the door. Driven by a need that had no anchor in logic or rational thought, he ran outside. He hit the curb just as Gus's Chevy pulled out of the drop-off area and cut into the heavy stream of traffic.

"Dammit!"

With utter ruthlessness, he commandeered a cab that was emptying its passengers curbside.

"I need to catch the dark green Chevy that just pulled away. Let's go."

"No, no, mister," the swarthy driver protested, gesturing to the long line of waiting cabs at the far end of the terminal. "I must go to the line's end. It is the rule."

"We're breaking the rules—" Jack skimmed the badge pinned to the man's shirt "—Mustafa."

Emptying his wallet, he thrust a wad of bills into the cabbie's hand. Without so much as a blink, the driver pocketed the bills and opened the passenger door.

"A dark green Chevy, you say. It is done."

The cab left the pickup area with a squeal of its tires that would have done Angela proud. Jack leaned forward, his gaze narrowed on the six lanes clogged with bumper-to-bumper rush-hour traffic. The slow pace both aided and frustrated the pursuit. To his intense relief, he caught a glimpse of the Chevy a half mile or so ahead. As much as Mustafa tried, though, he couldn't maneuver his cab any closer to the quarry.

Angela, on the other hand, weaved through miniscule openings in the traffic with seemingly effortless skill. It was that damned lug-nut school of driving she'd attended, Jack thought savagely as the dark green sedan pulled farther and farther away.

The short stretch of Memorial Parkway between National Airport and the turnoff for the Fourteenth Street Bridge seemed endless. Traffic slowed to a crawl as it approached the exit, then stopped completely.

Relief spiked through Jack when he caught sight of the Chevy in the lines of vehicles trying to feed onto the bridge ramp. His relief plummeted into chagrin, however, when the sedan slipped through impossible openings and inched its way up the ramp ahead of the other vehicles.

Leaving Mustafa shaking his head at the foibles of his passenger, Jack thrust open the door and dodged through the stalled traffic. The grassy verge beside the parkway allowed him more freedom of movement. In mere moments, he was up the ramp.

A chill wind off the Potomac knifed into his lungs. Exhaust fumes from the idling vehicles stung his eyes. Drivers' heads turned. Ignoring everything but the dark green sedan now only a few yards ahead, Jack twisted through a narrow passage of protruding side mirrors and extended bumpers. His only thought was to catch up with Angela.

He might have known she couldn't be caught.

As she'd informed him during his brief stint as a driver-in-training, a good driver always knows what's behind, beside and ahead. She'd shoved the Chevy into park, threw open the door, and jumped out of the vehicle before Jack was within twenty yards of the Chevy. The wind tossed her hair into a dark cloud as she ran to meet him.

"Jack! What's the matter? Oh, God, there hasn't been another disaster, has there?"

She threw herself into his arms, her frantic hands clutching at his suit sleeves. Head back, she searched his face for signs of injury.

"Your plane didn't blow up, did it? Terrorists didn't take over the terminal?"

"No," he panted, more winded than he wanted to admit from his headlong run. "No terrorists."

"Then what?" she demanded. "What?"

"I love you."

"*What?*"

At the look in her astounded eyes, Jack regained his breath and lost it again in the same instant.

"I love you," he repeated. "I love you here. Now. Forever. I'm not leaving Washington without you. I'm not leaving at all, if that's what you want."

"But... But..."

A horn sounded an impatient tattoo somewhere behind them. Jack didn't pay it any attention. Neither did the motorists who'd climbed out of their cars to gawk at the scene taking place in the middle of the bridge.

"No buts, sweetheart. No maybes. Please, Angela, make your mother and me happy. Marry me. Today. Tomorrow."

"I...I can't!"

His heart dropped clear through the bridge into the cold gray waters of the Potomac. Then Angela rose up on the tips of her sneakered toes and locked her arms around his neck.

"I can't marry you...not until we arrange to rent Gus's longest limo and Aunt Helen bakes the cannolis for the reception and Uncle Guido prints the fliers for the ceremony at Saint Ignacio's and...Michael agrees to sing at the ceremony."

Grinning, Jack tightened his arms and lifted her to his heart. "How long will all that take?"

"Not long," she answered, joyous laughter filling her voice. "Not with my mother orchestrating events."

Then she pulled his mouth down to hers.

# *Epilogue*

"Lucy!"

At the high-pitched, excited squeal, Lucy Falco's head shot up. Shoving away from her desk, she hurried into Gulliver's Travels' front office.

"What's the matter?"

The silver-haired Tiffany Tarrington Toulouse jumped up, waving a reservation form excitedly.

"Wait until you hear about the call I just got!"

Relieved that the building wasn't on fire or the office being burgled by another trio of bumbling thieves, Lucy dragged in a calming breath.

"It was Dr. Merritt," Tiffany exclaimed. "Do you remember that deluxe package I put together for his trip to Washington? The one he made me cancel?"

"Yes."

"He's just requested that we arrange another package with Top Hat Limousine Service at full, undiscounted rates."

"You're kidding!"

"No, look!"

The other travel agents crowded as Tiffany read the list of requirements in a bubbling, delighted voice.

"He wants their longest presidential stretch limo. *Not* number 286, because it's a slug."

"What?"

"That's what he said. Dom Pérignon '86, *not* '83. A single red rose in a silver vase. And—" she squinted at her scribbled notes "—a tape that includes every song ever recorded by Enrico Caruso, Mario Lanza and Placido Pavarotti."

"I think that's Luciano Pavarotti," one of the other agents put in.

Tiffany flapped a beringed hand. "Whoever."

"Do you have any idea what this is all about?" Lucy asked, reaching for the pink sheet.

"You're not going to believe this," the older woman predicted, a wide grin lighting her face. "He's taking his bride on a moonlight tour of Washington before they leave for their honeymoon."

"His bride!"

"He's getting married tomorrow. He said he was giving himself a delayed Valentine's Day present."

A stunned silence descended, broken only by Tiffany's merry, tinkling laughter.

"Can you believe it? Five holidays in five months, followed by five honeymoon packages. Gulliver's Travels has a perfect string going!"

"It certainly seems so," Lucy agreed faintly.

"Well, I'm not going to break the streak," Tiffany declared with a grin. "As soon as I make this reservation, I'm going to call Humphrey. He's only a child, of course, a mere fifty-one, but the man does possess the cutest buns I've seen in many a year. Besides which, he worships me. He positively worships me."

She snatched up a calendar filled with vivid pictures of European cities and flipped the page.

"Let's see, what's next? Aha! Saint Patrick's Day! That will do. That will do nicely."

Shooing her co-workers aside, she marched to her computer terminal. The other agents gaped at her, then turned thunderstruck faces to their office manager. Her dark eyes dancing, Lucy smiled.

"Tiffany Tarrington Toulouse and Humphrey Huffmeister on an Irish holiday honeymoon. It's perfect. Perfect."

*     *     *     *     *

TRACI ON THE SPOT          BY TRACI

# 1

→ ←

Morgan Brigham slowly set down his coffee cup on the kitchen table and stared at the comic strip in the center of his paper. It was nestled in among approximately twenty others that were spread out across two pages. But this was the only one he made a point of reading faithfully each morning at breakfast.

This was the only one that mirrored *her* life.

He read each panel twice, as if he couldn't trust his own eyes. But he could. It was there, in black and white.

Morgan folded the paper slowly, thoughtfully, his mind not on his task. So Traci was getting engaged.

The realization gnawed at the lining of his stomach. He hadn't a clue as to why.

He had even less of a clue why he did what he did next.

Abandoning his coffee, now cool, and the newspaper, and ignoring the fact that this was going to make him late for the office, Morgan went to get a sheet of stationery from the den.

He didn't have much time.

Traci Richardson stared at the last frame she had just drawn. Debating, she glanced at the creature sprawled out on the kitchen floor.

"What do you think, Jeremiah? Too blunt?"

The dog, part bloodhound, part mutt, idly looked up from his rawhide bone at the sound of his name. Jeremiah gave her a look she felt free to interpret as ambivalent.

"Fine help you are. What if Daniel actually reads this and puts two and two together?"

Not that there was all that much chance that the man who had proposed to her, the very prosperous and busy Dr. Daniel Thane, would actually see the comic strip she drew for a living. Not unless the strip was taped to a bicuspid he was examining. Lately Daniel had gotten so busy he'd stopped reading anything but the morning headlines of the *Times*.

Still, you never knew. "I don't want to hurt his feelings," Traci continued, using Jeremiah as a sounding board. "It's just that Traci is overwhelmed by Donald's proposal and, see, she thinks the ring is going to swallow her up." To prove her point, Traci held up the drawing for the dog to view.

This time, he didn't even bother to lift his head.

Traci stared moodily at the small velvet box on the kitchen counter. It had sat there since Daniel had asked her to marry him last Sunday. Even if Daniel never read her comic strip, he was going to suspect something eventually. The very fact that she hadn't grabbed the ring from his hand and slid it onto her finger should have told him that she had doubts about their union.

Traci sighed. Daniel was a catch by any definition. So what was her problem? She kept waiting to be struck by that sunny ray of happiness. Daniel said he wanted to take care of her, to fulfill her every wish. And he was even willing to let her think about it before she gave him her answer.

Guilt nibbled at her. She should be dancing up and down, not wavering like a weather vane in a gale.

Pronouncing the strip completed, she scribbled her signature in the corner of the last frame and then sighed. Another week's work put to bed. She glanced at the pile of mail on the counter. She'd been bringing it in steadily from the mailbox since Monday, but the stack had gotten no farther than her kitchen. Sorting letters seemed the least heinous of all the annoying chores that faced her.

Traci paused as she noted a long envelope. Morgan Brigham. Why would Morgan be writing to her?

Curious, she tore open the envelope and quickly scanned the short note inside.

Dear Traci,

I'm putting the summerhouse up for sale. Thought you might want to come up and see it one more time before it goes up on the block. Or make a bid for it yourself. If memory serves, you once said you wanted to buy it. Either way, let me know. My number's on the card.

Take care,
Morgan

P.S. Got a kick out of *Traci on the Spot* this week.

Traci folded the letter. He read her strip. She hadn't known that. A feeling of pride silently coaxed a smile to her lips. After a beat, though, the rest of his note seeped into her consciousness. He was selling the house.

The summerhouse. A faded white building with brick

trim. Suddenly, memories flooded her mind. Long, lazy afternoons that felt as if they would never end.

*Morgan.*

She looked at the far wall in the family room. There was a large framed photograph of her and Morgan standing before the summerhouse. Traci and Morgan. Morgan and Traci. Back then, it seemed their lives had been permanently intertwined. A bittersweet feeling of loss passed over her.

Traci quickly pulled the telephone over to her on the counter and tapped out the number on the keypad.

* * * * *

*Look for TRACI ON THE SPOT*
*by Marie Ferrarella, coming to*
*Silhouette YOURS TRULY*
*in March 1997.*

*At last the wait is over...*
In March
*New York Times* bestselling author

# NORA ROBERTS

will bring us the latest from the Stanislaskis as
Natasha's now very grown-up stepdaughter,
Freddie, and Rachel's very sexy brother-in-law
Nick discover that love is worth waiting for in

## WAITING FOR NICK

Silhouette Special Edition #1088

and in April
visit Natasha and Rachel again—or meet them
for the first time—in

# The Stanislaski Sisters

containing TAMING NATASHA
and FALLING FOR RACHEL

Available wherever Silhouette books are sold.

NRSS

# MILLION DOLLAR SWEEPSTAKES
## OFFICIAL RULES
### NO PURCHASE NECESSARY TO ENTER

1. To enter, follow the directions published. Method of entry may vary. For eligibility, entries must be received no later than March 31, 1998. No liability is assumed for printing errors, lost, late, non-delivered or misdirected entries.

   To determine winners, the sweepstakes numbers assigned to submitted entries will be compared against a list of randomly, preselected prize winning numbers. In the event all prizes are not claimed via the return of prize winning numbers, random drawings will be held from among all other entries received to award unclaimed prizes.

2. Prize winners will be determined no later than June 30, 1998. Selection of winning numbers and random drawings are under the supervision of D. L. Blair, Inc., an independent judging organization whose decisions are final. Limit: one prize to a family or organization. No substitution will be made for any prize, except as offered. Taxes and duties on all prizes are the sole responsibility of winners. Winners will be notified by mail. Odds of winning are determined by the number of eligible entries distributed and received.

3. Sweepstakes open to residents of the U.S. (except Puerto Rico), Canada and Europe who are 18 years of age or older, except employees and immediate family members of Torstar Corp., D. L. Blair, Inc., their affiliates, subsidiaries, and all other agencies, entities, and persons connected with the use, marketing or conduct of this sweepstakes. All applicable laws and regulations apply. Sweepstakes offer void wherever prohibited by law. Any litigation within the province of Quebec respecting the conduct and awarding of a prize in this sweepstakes must be submitted to the Régie des alcools, des courses et des jeux. In order to win a prize, residents of Canada will be required to correctly answer a time-limited arithmetical skill-testing question to be administered by mail.

4. Winners of major prizes (Grand through Fourth) will be obligated to sign and return an Affidavit of Eligibility and Release of Liability within 30 days of notification. In the event of non-compliance within this time period or if a prize is returned as undeliverable, D. L. Blair, Inc. may at its sole discretion, award that prize to an alternate winner. By acceptance of their prize, winners consent to use of their names, photographs or other likeness for purposes of advertising, trade and promotion on behalf of Torstar Corp., its affiliates and subsidiaries, without further compensation unless prohibited by law. Torstar Corp. and D. L. Blair, Inc., their affiliates and subsidiaries are not responsible for errors in printing of sweepstakes and prize winning numbers. In the event a duplication of a prize winning number occurs, a random drawing will be held from among all entries received with that prize winning number to award that prize.

5. This sweepstakes is presented by Torstar Corp., its subsidiaries and affiliates in conjunction with book, merchandise and/or product offerings. The number of prizes to be awarded and their value are as follows: Grand Prize — $1,000,000 (payable at $33,333.33 a year for 30 years); First Prize — $50,000; Second Prize — $10,000; Third Prize — $5,000; 3 Fourth Prizes — $1,000 each; 10 Fifth Prizes — $250 each; 1,000 Sixth Prizes — $10 each. Values of all prizes are in U.S. currency. Prizes in each level will be presented in different creative executions, including various currencies, vehicles, merchandise and travel. Any presentation of a prize level in a currency other than U.S. currency represents an approximate equivalent to the U.S. currency prize for that level, at that time. Prize winners will have the opportunity of selecting any prize offered for that level; however, the actual non U.S. currency equivalent prize if offered and selected, shall be awarded at the exchange rate existing at 3:00 P.M. New York time on March 31, 1998. A travel prize option, if offered and selected by winner, must be completed within 12 months of selection and is subject to: traveling companion(s) completing and returning of a Release of Liability prior to travel; and hotel and flight accommodations availability. For a current list of all prize options offered within prize levels, send a self-addressed, stamped envelope (WA residents need not affix postage) to: MILLION DOLLAR SWEEPSTAKES Prize Options, P.O. Box 4456, Blair, NE 68009-4456, USA.

6. For a list of prize winners (available after July 31, 1998) send a separate, stamped, self-addressed envelope to: MILLION DOLLAR SWEEPSTAKES Winners, P.O. Box 4459, Blair, NE 68009-4459, USA.

# As seen on TV!
# *Free Gift Offer*

With a Free Gift proof-of-purchase from any Silhouette® book, you can receive a beautiful cubic zirconia pendant.

This gorgeous marquise-shaped stone is a genuine cubic zirconia—accented by an 18" gold tone necklace.

(Approximate retail value $19.95)

# Send for yours today...
## compliments of *Silhouette*®

To receive your free gift, a cubic zirconia pendant, send us one original proof-of-purchase, photocopies not accepted, from the back of any Silhouette Romance™, Silhouette Desire®, Silhouette Special Edition®, Silhouette Intimate Moments® or Silhouette Yours Truly™ title available in February, March and April at your favorite retail outlet, together with the Free Gift Certificate, plus a check or money order for $1.65 U.S./$2.15 CAN. (do not send cash) to cover postage and handling, payable to Silhouette Free Gift Offer. We will send you the specified gift. Allow 6 to 8 weeks for delivery. Offer good until April 30, 1997 or while quantities last. Offer valid in the U.S. and Canada only.

## *Free Gift Certificate*

Name: _____

Address: _____

City: _____ State/Province: _____ Zip/Postal Code: _____

Mail this certificate, one proof-of-purchase and a check or money order for postage and handling to: SILHOUETTE FREE GIFT OFFER 1997. In the U.S.: 3010 Walden Avenue, P.O. Box 9077, Buffalo NY 14269-9077. In Canada: P.O. Box 613, Fort Erie, Ontario L2Z 5X3.

---

## FREE GIFT OFFER                                              084-KFD
ONE PROOF-OF-PURCHASE
To collect your fabulous FREE GIFT, a cubic zirconia pendant, you must include this original proof-of-purchase for each gift with the properly completed Free Gift Certificate.

084-KFI

# COMING NEXT MONTH

# You're About to Become a *Privileged Woman*

## Reap the rewards of fabulous free gifts and benefits with proofs-of-purchase from Silhouette and Harlequin books

# Pages & Privileges™

It's our way of thanking you for buying our books at your favorite retail stores.

**PROOF OF PURCHASE**

SIM-PP22

Offer expires March 31, 1997

## Harlequin and Silhouette— the most privileged readers in the world!

For more information about Harlequin and Silhouette's PAGES & PRIVILEGES program call the Pages & Privileges Benefits Desk: 1-503-794-2499

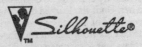

*Silhouette*®

SIM-PP22